CASUAL

By Gavin Anderson

Low Life

To anyone who has stood their ground
on the terraces

Casual (pbk)

© Gavin Anderson, 1996

ISBN 1 898928 20 7

Published by S.T. Publishing, Scotland.
Printed by Progressive, England.

This book is a work of fiction. The characters and
events in this novel are purely imaginary.

Low Life is an imprint of
S.T. PUBLISHING
P.O. Box 12, Dunoon, Argyll. PA23 7BQ. Scotland.
As of September, 1996, we will be at a new address. If you want to
contact us before that date please write to the Dunoon address above.
After that date please contact us at
S.T. Publishing,
P.O. Box 12, Lockerbie, Dumfries. DG11 3BW. Scotland.

Gavin Anderson first became a casual while living in Edinburgh. He now lives in London.

CHAPTER ONE

COME ON ARSENAL! COME ON ARSENAL! the packed North Bank chanted as the Arsenal team mounted yet another attack on the Chelsea goal.

GOAL!

The ground erupted in cheers.

TWO NIL FOR THE ARSENAL, TWO NIL FOR THE ARSENAL!

There was no way back for Chelsea now.

High on the North Bank, Lee Jones scanned the heaving terracing. His eyes stopped on two Arsenal fans dressed in Lacoste and Diadora. "C'mon lads, there's two of 'em down there!"

He led his mob through the crowd, pushing and shoving towards their unsuspecting prey. High on drugs and adrenaline, Lee stormed forward yelling, "C'mon Arsenal! Let's fucking go!"

The two Arsenal boys spun around to face their rivals. "Yeah, c'mon you Chelsea mugs, let's do it!", said one, regretting it immediately when he realised that the other Arsenal fans standing around him didn't want to know.

The crowd pushed back as the Chelsea lads surged towards them. The grin on Lee's face grew as he crashed his fist into the nearest fan's face. Lee felt the blow jar his muscles as it buckled his victim's nose and the blood seeped through his fingers. As the victim slumped in agony, Lee kicked out, landing his Gazelle in the soft stomach of the decked casual. As he aimed another kick, he laughed and glanced over his shoulder to see the rest of the firm wading into the other Arsenal casual. Muffled moans from the two casuals on the receiving end were drowned out by the chanting of the firm - CHELSEA! CHELSEA!

Kevin Murray surveyed the scene with some worry. "Leave 'em! They've 'ad enough!"

"Fuck off, Kev! We ain't started yet!" Lee snarled as he aimed another Gazelle at the limp body in front of him.

Kevin looked around in despair and spotted the coppers' helmets moving slowly towards them. "Move lads! It's the Old Bill!"

Kevin sighed thankfully as the mob split in different directions and disappeared into the crowd.

By the time DI Welsh of the Fulham CID reached the scene there was no sign of the Chelsea mob. Just the aftermath of the sickening and bloody attack. The two youths were bleeding badly and it was hard to tell if there were any knife wounds or not. He watched as the uniform lads helped the battered bodies to their feet and escorted them to the running track below. *One day, Jones, just one day.*

Lee, now at the other side of the terracing, smiled to himself as he watched the wounded Arsenal casuals being stretchered around the pitch to the chant of CHELSEA AGGRO! courtesy of the Chelsea fans massed in the Clock End. *Another away win*, Lee thought smugly to himself.

Lee and Kevin had been Chelsea fans all their lives. They knew Chelsea had one of the best firms in

England - if not the best - and they had always wanted to be a part of it as soon as they were old enough. Neither him nor Kevin needed much encouragement when they were faced with their first ruck when they were only 15 or 16. It wasn't as though they were involved every week initially, but they had been drawn in by the exhilaration of those first blows and the jubilation afterwards as the sore losers were escorted out the Shed. As the years progressed they got involved more regularly, inside and outside the grounds where Chelsea played. Now Lee had his own firm, with Kevin as his right-hand man. Lee was known by the main faces at Chelsea and was well respected by those impressed with what they saw. Dressed in nothing but the best from Stone Island to Ralph Lauren, he was every bit the natural leader.

The crowd streamed out of Highbury and Lee blended in with the jubilant Arsenal fans. His smile was for a different reason, another result for his gang of casuals. His only concern was his old schoolmate, Kev, and his attempt to stop the attack when he thought the enemy had had enough. In Lee's estimation, there could be no limits to the violence if they wanted to be the top dogs. As he continued to walk towards Finsbury Park tube station, he felt a tap on his shoulder.

"Lee! Lee! Hang on!"

"Awright, Tel."

"Yeah, brilliant result, eh?"

"Well, our honour is still intact if that's what you're talking about," Lee replied, knowing that turning over two Arsenal boys was hardly major league stuff.

"What's got into Kev?" Tel asked. "He looked like an amateur up on the terracing this afternoon."

"Kev's awright. Someone had to keep an eye out for the coppers," Lee said defensively.

"Aw, c'mon Lee. You know what I'm talking about. This ain't the first time this has happened!"

"Leave it out, Tel, will ya!"

Terry grabbed Lee's sleeve, bringing him to a stand still. Lee looked at the hand that held him and then glared at the owner.

Terry dropped his hand before saying, "Lee, face facts. Kev's losing his bottle. He's chickening out on us!"

"Tel, I ain't gonna say this again. Kev is awright! Now let's get going before we get sussed."

Lee once again headed towards the tube station and Terry followed in behind him, angry that Lee couldn't see what was happening to Kevin, or more to the point, didn't want to see. Terry thought that Kevin was becoming an embarrassment. It wouldn't be long before Kevin made them a laughing stock, and Terry wanted something done about it before it was too late. But what?

Kevin could just make out Lee and Terry up ahead and couldn't work out what was going on. It wasn't like Terry to have a go at Lee - nobody had a go at Lee, apart from him. He couldn't get any closer as the jostling, joking Arsenal fans packed the pavement, putting more bodies in between them.

"Damn it!"

"What was that, Kev?"

"Huh, nothin' John. Let's get out of here. The sight of all these happy Gooners is making me sick!"

John laughed and looked around for the rest of the firm. Ian and Mad Mike were on the opposite side of the street. "'Ere, Kev, watch Mike!"

Kevin looked over to where John was pointing. Mike was clipping the heels of the Arsenal fans in front of him, making them stumble and stagger into the heaving mass directly in front of them. Every time an embarrassed fan looked around to see who was tripping him, Mike just side stepped out of the way, leaving innocent fans to collect the dirty looks and comments.

Kevin laughed. "Typical! No wonder he gets called Mad Mike!"

"Yeah! Look at Ian, he's struggling to keep a straight face!"

The pair of them laughed again as they entered the tube station.

CHAPTER TWO

"Yo, Lee."

"Awright, Kev, mate."

The two friends met around the corner from their local nightclub on the Streatham High Road.

"Got the gear?" Kev asked.

"Yeah, just picked it up. The geezer's havin' a laugh. He tried to charge me nearly double what we agreed on!"

"Greedy bastard!"

"I put 'im right though." Lee rubbed the knuckles on his right hand and Kevin grinned. "'Ere Kev, can you take some of it off my hands? I ended up with a bit more than normal. Lee pulled out a clear plastic bag stuffed full of tiny foil packets and smaller sealed plastic bags containing white tablets.

Kevin's eyes almost popped out of his head. "Christ! You must've forked out a small fortune for that lot!"

"Well, I kinda struck up a new deal after he agreed on the original asking price."

"Excellent! Yeah, I'll take some of it off you. This place should be begging for this stuff tonight."

"How?"

"That new DJ starts tonight and he's shit hot so everyone heading this way."

"A bit more pocket money for us then, eh? Let's get going."

They strolled around the corner and walked towards the club. There was already a small queue, but they just went straight to the front and the bouncers automatically opened the doors to them, greeting Lee and Kevin by name. They swaggered in, ignoring the cashier. She glanced up at them and then moved her glance to the bouncers, but they just turned back to doors.

The two lads stopped just inside the door and surveyed the scene in front of them. The place was virtually full already, and Lee smiled at the thought of the money he'd make from the drugs in his pocket. Lee unzipped his tan suede Armani jacket and headed for the bar. Kevin followed suit, conscious of the fact that his old Mau Mau jacket was no match for Lee's new Armani.

"Flash cunt," he muttered under his breath as a blonde girl stalked towards to Lee.

"Awright, Shaz?" Lee smiled at her.

Sharon stood with her hands on her hips, defiantly. "Is that all you've gotta say? I've been waitin' for a call for days now!"

"I've been busy," Lee snapped back and walked on.

Sharon's shoulders slumped and her hands fell from her Katherine Hamnett jeans. She shook her head, knowing Lee would never listen to her.

Kevin smiled at her and walked past as well, leaving Sharon to spin around and tail after them.

As the three of them neared the bar, punters turned to look, but soon moved away when they saw who was passing them. The barman ignored the other waiting customers and served Lee and his mate their usual bottles of Sol. He nodded in Sharon's direction, but his eyes were still on Lee as if it was Lee's call whether Sharon got a drink or not.

"Get her whatever she wants." Lee turned and leaned on the bar to look around the club again. The smoky atmosphere hid the clubbers apprehensive looks along with their cheap High Street labels.

Within minutes the rest of the firm were milling around, asking what was on the cards for the night ahead. Lee grinned and told them to keep cool.

Sharon shook her head and Lee threw her a fiery look. She sat herself down on a stool and resigned herself to her boyfriend being "busy" again tonight.

Lee looked towards Kevin, his right hand man, who launched into the tactics for the night ahead. The firm listened intently. Kevin informed them that a mob were coming over from Tottenham to try to do the club. Excitement spread through the ranks and everyone started looking about to see if any of the Yids had already invaded their territory.

Lee noticed this. "Right lads, just keep your eyes open and I'll give you the nod. And try and lighten my load." He handed out a few acid and Ecstasy tablets to each of them and they stuffed them into their pockets with zero fuss. "Remember and sell them - don't give them away!"

They nodded and then disappeared among the enthusiastic clubbers.

A young lad in Armani jeans and a Duffer sweatshirt appeared from the smoky dancefloor and approached Lee and Kevin. Lee looked him up and down as the young lad looked about nervously, his eyes slightly bulging and bloodshot. He shoved his hand into his pocket and pulled out a crumpled £20 note. Kevin offered a foil packet and a white Ecstasy tablet and the lad took the Ecstasy. Kevin took the money from him and he moved back into the smoke. Kevin smiled. "Like taking candy from a baby!"

"Too right, Kev," said Lee before attracting the barman's attention. "Two more bottles mate!"

Sharon looked over, hoping Lee hadn't forgotten her already. He just turned to talk to Kevin again. She opened her mouth, but shut it again, thinking better of speaking her mind to Lee. She slipped off the stool and went in search of her friends.

Kevin noticed her walking away and nudged Lee who looked over his shoulder at the retreating slim, long legged figure.

"She'll be back!" Lee said.

It wasn't long before she was, with some of her friends hanging back slightly.

"Lee?"

Lee leaned on the bar and hoped she wasn't going to make scene. *No doubt those mates of hers have put her up to this. Bleedin' hell, this is the last thing I need tonight - a nagging girlfriend!*

"Lee?"

"What?"

"Lee, you do still fancy me don't ya?"

"Yeah."

"Well, when am I gonna see ya again?"

"I'm here ain't I?"

She was starting to irritate him.

"I mean alone, just us, together."

"Oh, is that all!" He was trying not to lose his temper with her, but it wasn't easy. "I'll see. I'll phone you."

13

"Phone me?!" She was shrieking and her eyes were blazing. "Phone me?!"

"Will you calm down!" Lee snapped at her, hoping she wasn't drawing any attention to them. "I said I'll phone, so I'll phone. I'm busy these days, you know!"

"Yeah, busy with *that* football team of yours! Is *that* team more important than me or what?"

Lee glared at her angrily. "I'll phone you!"

Kevin looked around at them, only to find Lee's glare transfer to him. The look in Lee's eyes made Kevin look away.

Sharon, determined not to back down, took an airy stance. "Yeah, well you just do that, but I can't say if I'll be in. I'm busy too y'know!"

"You'll be there." Lee turned away.

She just stared at his back, angry because he didn't pay her any attention and angry because she knew he was right. She would be there whenever he phoned.

She walked away to join her friends and Lee glanced around in time to see them staring at him while Sharon gestured wildy with her arms. He had to smile.

Lee and Kevin had moved to the side of the dancefloor when John came over and told them about a commotion at the front door between the bouncers and a mob of lads.

A surge of adrenaline coursed through Lee's veins as he straightened his back. "Come on, firm up! The Yids are here!"

A mob of 30 or so Chelsea ran towards the entrance, scattering unsuspecting clubbers as they did so. The firm's hearts pounded to the beat of the music as their alcohol-fuelled bodies faced up to the Tottenham mob who had burst past the struggling bouncers and were pouring into the club.

A tear gas canister exploded in front of Chelsea, who momentarily backed off, covering their faces. The Spurs mob then steamed in with baseball bats and Stanley knives.

Lee moved in, smashing his beer bottle into a leading Tottenham fan's face. He smirked as the punctured face spewed blood and the owner squealed in pain. Lee's smirk then turned into a manic grin as he lashed out with his flick knife. It was kicking off all over the club's dancefloor now, and the sound of breaking glass and the screams of panic stricken girls were music to his ears.

A Tottenham fan lunged at Lee with a blade and it ripped through his Ralph Lauren shirt.

"You fuckin' bastard!" Lee raged as he punched the bloke to the ground.

Kevin ran over to help Lee as the bloke started to struggle. The other Tottenham lads were starting to back off into the street, leaving their mate to face the consequences.

"Hold 'im down Kev!"

"What?"

"You 'eard!"

Kevin tried to force the Yid to stay still, but he still tried to grapple with them both.

John headed in their direction to see what was happening.

"Oi, John, give us a hand!" Lee snarled as John helped pin the squirming man down on the floor with his arms above his head. "Smile, you Yid bastard!"

Lee opened the panic stricken man's left cheek with his knife. "Smile forever!"

He did the same to the right cheek. The Tottenham fan screamed in agony. Lee stood up and aimed his Ellesse trainer at the man's groin to open up the cuts, and then walked away smiling.

Kevin backed away in shock and stared in amazement at Lee. He realised his mouth was hanging open and he shut it consciously with a click of teeth.

Lee smiling smugly to himself, swaggered over to Kevin. "Awright, mate?"

"That was way over Lee, well out of order."

"Fuck off Kev, look at my shirt! Anyway, what's got into you recently?"

"What's got into me? Have a look at yourself. It's just meant to be a laugh all of this, but only I don't see many people laughin' anymore!"

"Well, I made that bastard laugh and he'll be smiling about it for the rest of his life!"

Kevin started for the door. "I'm off home before the Old Bill get here."

As he walked out he noticed Sharon who was standing by the door with her mates. She shrugged her shoulders as he stepped into the cool night air.

"What's eatin' him then?" asked Terry, a smartly dressed youth from Woolwich, who was standing behind Lee. "Lost his bottle? I don't know why you put up with him, Lee!"

"Look, he's awright! He's got more bottle that all the rest of you put together! Now come on, let's make sure that no one saw anything, and then get out of here before the coppers get 'ere!"

The firm split up and made their way around the small clusters of stunned punters, making sure each and every one of them was ready to do a good impression of the three wise monkeys.

Lee sauntered over to where Sharon and her friends were standing. "Come on Shaz, you ready?"

Sharon just glanced at him and turned back to her chatting friends.

"Suit yourself, see ya later!" He brushed past her as he made his way to the door and noticed her turning to follow him.

"I'm sorry, Lee." She linked her arm through Lee's as they walked onto the street.

"Lee, why did you do it?" she asked as they started to head home. "It's true what Kev said, it was out of order."

"Leave it out will ya, Shaz. I'm sick of hearing about it. It's all everyone's talked about."

"I'm frightened."

He stopped and looked down at her worried face. "Don't be."

He eased her into a nearby bus shelter. Her lips met his, their probing tongues touching. She felt his dick harden and she unzipped his jeans to release his straining manhood.

This is the life, thought Lee as he watched the top of Sharon's head bob up and down at his crotch. *I can't go wrong!*

CHAPTER THREE

DI Welsh stood looking out of the window with his hands clasped behind his back. He had always wanted to be a policeman; always wanted to chase and collar all of life's baddies.

He joined the Met after leaving school and pounded the beat for several years, never considering moving upwards through the ranks. He enjoyed being a plod in uniform, and it wasn't until he got married that he thought about promotion. With a wife, house and the patter of tiny feet, he had to think about his future. He managed to get on a small squad of uniform who were seconded to CID to assist in some undercover work. He excelled himself so much that the DCI requested that Welsh stay with CID. Welsh never stood still after that - it was onwards and upwards as far as his career with the Force was concerned.

He was happy with his present post of DI at Fulham. He had been there for a few years now. With management being thinned, he had to keep in front to keep on top, and if he could nail the Chelsea hooligans it could be his chance to be short-listed for promotion. "I am going to nail these bloody hooligans!" he muttered to himself as he walked to the briefing room. "They are NOT going to get the better of me!"

His squad of Detective Sergeants and Constables sat around in silence, glancing at one another nervously. DI Welsh slowly turned to face them. "Do any of you know what this is?" He held up a white piece of card the size of a credit card. "Answer me someone! Do you?"

He was trying to contain his temper. The piece of card had YOU HAVE BEEN NOMINATED AND DEALT WITH BY CHELSEA THUGS emblazoned on it.

"It's a calling card, Guv." It was a unison of several of them.

"That's right, a calling card!" He was turning crimson with anger. "I want these young upstarts stopped and stopped now!" He was struggling to control his temper. "Now, this was found in the nightclub on the Streatham High Road after the assault last night. The club is a local to a person called Lee Jones. A 26 year old from Streatham and a well known Chelsea hooligan. He seems to instigate a lot of the terrace and street disorder both at Chelsea and England games abroad."

He paused to look at the faces in the room to make sure that they were keeping up with him and following the copy papers he'd already handed to them. "Last night some madman viciously assaulted a youth from North London in this nightclub. However, as usual, nobody saw anything. So we are to assume Jones had some involvement due to the fact that the victim is a Tottenham Hotspur fan, and as we all know the two sets of fans do not get on."

Welsh was now pacing up and down the room. "It's obvious to everyone in this room that the quicker young Jones is off the streets and away from Stamford Bridge the better."

He stopped pacing. His piercing eyes went from one person to the next. "Has anyone got any ideas about how we can break his gang and collar Jones?"

"Guv?"

"Sergeant MacKenzie?"

"Well, Jones hangs around with a lad called Kevin Murray. They grew up together. The word on the streets is that Murray is getting alienated from the casual scene now that the violence is escalating. Maybe we could watch him?"

"Hmm, you think this lad may be running scared then? Looking for a way out perhaps?"

"Maybe not right now, Guv, but he may not be prepared to take much more."

"The Football Intelligence Unit have a covert officer in with Chelsea at the moment. Maybe we can use him to niggle Murray." The thought of getting one more nail in Jones's coffin pleased DI Welsh greatly. "Right then, Sergeant, get as much as you can on this lad and see if the FIU can get their man to help. Keep him under observation. We may have to pay him a visit."

Lee lay on his back with his hands behind his head. A smile creased his face as he thought about the successful time he had had the previous day - humiliating the Gooners in their own end, the ruck in the club, the smile he had put on that Yid's face, and then the time he had spent with Sharon.

"Shit, she's good, bloody good," he said aloud. Lee thought a lot of Sharon. She was good looking, she loved him and she was a damn good fuck.

"Ah fuck!" he moaned as he felt a stirring in his groin. He shook his head and frowned. He liked

20

Sharon a lot, but he wouldn't dare let her know that -
there was his reputation to think of!

His grinning face turned into a puzzled face as his
thoughts turned to his best friend. *What the fuck's got
into Kevin? Maybe Terry was right, maybe Kev has
lost his bottle.* He sat up trying to think what had got
into his best mate, his right hand man, the person he
had grown up with. He was more like a brother than a
friend.

Even when they were kids, nicking sweets from the
corner shop, Kevin was there, joining in. The
schoolboy pranks against the teachers and other kids.
Kevin did things off his own back then. Lee thought
about the time at school when they were caught
smoking in the bogs and bullying the wimps for cash.
Kevin told the headmaster to "Fuck off" and started to
smash up the office.

Lee laughed to himself. *Those were the days! The
good ol' days! But what about now?* It was starting to
piss Lee off. *I'm gonna have a word with him!*

He reached over and picked up the phone and dialled
Kevin's number.

"Hello?"

"Awright Kev, it's Lee."

"Morning Lee. This is a bit early for you innit?
You at Sharon's?"

"Nah, I got a taxi back in the early hours. Left her
well fucked! Anyway, what are you up to today, got
any plans?"

"Not until tonight, why?"

"Wanna come over? We can make arrangements for
next week's match with Millwall and the England match
next month."

"Do you ever stop?"

"What do you mean?" asked Lee defensively.

"All this madness! Take last night, that lad's face! Why did you do it?"

"For fuck's sake Kev, not again! Listen, he's Spurs so he deserves it! Kev, the lads think your bottle's going - we've gotta talk about it."

"I bet it was Terry that said that!" Kev said, knowing full well that Terry resented his close friendship with Lee.

"What if it was?"

"That doesn't matter, you're just getting out of hand. I don't like what you're getting up to these days."

"Come on, Kev, you're going soft! What about when we were kids? We did everything together and now you're turning into a sap!"

"It was different then, we were kids. Everything was just a laugh and we only had our folks and the teachers pulling us up. But now it's getting serious and the Old Bill are on our tails."

"Fuck the Old Bill! You're not scared of them are you? C'mon Kev, you're the one who's getting out of hand!" Lee was straining to keep his cool.

"Alright! Alright! Calm down! I'll come over. I'll be there about lunchtime, see you then."

"Okay, see ya." Lee hung up the phone and shook his head. "What's got into him?" he muttered.

No sooner had he put it down and the phone started ringing again. "Hello?"

"Hiya, honey!"

"Awright, Shaz, surprised you're up so early."

Sharon giggled. "Oh lover, I'm still recovering! Lee, honey, is it okay for me to come over today?"

"Are you after more?" Lee asked jokingly. "Just can't get enough, eh?"

"That's right, I just can't help myself!"

"Yeah, come down whenever you want. Kev's coming down too."

Sharon's heart sank with disappointment, and her silence let Lee in on the secret.

"Is that a problem? Kev understands, he won't mind watching telly for an hour or so."

"Okay then, if you're sure," she said. "I'll be down soon. See ya!" She blew a few kisses down the phone.

"See ya, Shaz, bye." Lee smiled broadly at the thought of slipping between Sharon's thighs again.

CHAPTER FOUR

As Kevin sat on the top deck of the bus, thinking about the telephone conversation he had had with Lee, he felt someone sit next to him.

"Hiya, Kev."

"Awright Sharon. Where are you off to?"

"Same place as you."

"Oh right, he never said anything on the phone this morning."

"So it was you who was on the phone for so long. What were you two talking about?"

"Don't ask! He was still bragging about his exploits yesterday."

"Oh no!" Sharon cringed at the thought of the previous night. "It was 'orrible! I couldn't believe what he did to that bloke."

"I know, I'm trying to get him to cool it, but he won't listen to me."

"You too? I had a go at 'im last night, but he wasn't listenin'. I'm worried, Kevin. He was always wild, but never this bad. He never used to have this evil streak in him did he? You've known 'im for ages, what did 'e used to be like?"

"He always has been a bit violent. But, he had it under control. Well, sometimes."

"Sometimes? Like when?"

"When we were going through school, we were the bullies from beginning to end. You know the kinda things; slap the wimpy kids about, pull girls' pigtails! Then onto extorting money and ciggies and whatever else was going round. Just having a laugh really." He smiled as he reminisced. "Has he ever mentioned when we were mods?"

Sharon shook her head. When it came down to it, she knew very little about her boyfriend's past.

"No skinhead fucked with us! Even up Chelsea in the Shed when most of 'em were skins, we would walk about with our parkas on and they still accepted us. Down here in Streatham we used to command a bit of respect. We were the faces of the South London Mods."

Kevin felt proud about those days and he carried on. "There was this East London mod, a Glory Boy, and he used to say that if we had lived over the Mile End we could have been the new Twins! Can you believe it?! We were only having a laugh and people were actually scared and they respected us!" Kevin still hadn't got over that Krays comment.

"Some things never change!" said Sharon.

Kevin laughed. "Yeah, there was this time down at Brighton on the Bank Holiday when it all kicked off good style on the beach with the skinheads. Lee went mental. Fuck knows how many he floored. 'E didn't even stop when the coppers started appearing. Me and a few of the lads 'ad to pull 'im away. When we told 'im what had happened, he could hardly remember a thing about it. In fact, if it hadn't been for the blood all over 'is parka, I don't think he would've believed us."

"Do you reckon that's what happening now?"

"Nah, doubt it. Lee knows what's going on all right. 'E's gonna end up going for a stretch if he carries on."

"He frightens me sometimes. That psycho look he gets in this eyes." Sharon bit on her bottom lip to stop the tears.

Kevin felt sorry for her. He knew she was one hell of a sort and she deserved to be treated better. "But what can we do about it? None of the other lads think he's out of order. That bastard Terry thinks I'm losing my bottle."

"But you're being sensible, Kevin. The rest of 'em are just mindless idiots who would jump off a cliff if Lee told 'em to!"

The two of them started to laugh, but both knew that she was right. Kevin looked down onto the street below, thinking it was quiet for a Sunday. The road was empty apart from the panda car going in the opposite direction.

"Pigs!" he muttered as the police car passed the bus.

"What was that, Kevin?" Sharon said, not quite catching what he'd said.

"Nothing, just the Old Bill looking for trouble as usual."

The doorbell rang and Lee got up to answer the door. "Awright. I see you two met on the way."

"Hiya, hon." Sharon pecked him on the cheek. "Yeah, we met on the bus."

"Right then, let's get straight down to business," Lee said as they made their way down the hallway. "Sharon, love, be a good girl and make some coffee. Me and Kev have got a few things to discuss." Lee playfully slapped her bum.

Sharon giggled and wiggled her way towards the kitchen while the lads went into the living room. Kevin

26

looked around the familiar room and realised just how much paraphernalia Lee had gathered on Chelsea and the hooligan mobs associated with the club. The walls were covered in photos of Chelsea teams through the years, especially the Cup winning side. He also had bundles of programmes, and in the bookcase in the corner was a row of books about Chelsea FC as well as every book ever written about football hooliganism. And on top of the bookcase was a stack of scrap books, each one full of newspaper cuttings about football aggro - not only from Chelsea, but from all over the world.

"Right Kev, we've got Millwall at home on Saturday and the rumours 'ave it that they'll have about 400 lads. Seemingly they're gonna try and take the West Stand so everyone is gonna be there. Are you in?"

"Course I'm fuckin' in!" said Kev, annoyed that Lee even felt the need to ask. "I'm always there ain't I?"

"Well, recently a few of the lads are 'aving doubts about you, me included."

"Leave it out will ya, Lee! I ain't lost my bottle, I just think that everything is going a bit too far now. Especially you. Take last night - what you done to that Tottenham bloke was bang out of order."

"Fuck off, Kev! He deserved it! Anyway, that's in the past - just you make sure that you're all set for Saturday. I don't want the rest of the firm thinking you're going soft."

"As I said, I'll be there."

"Good, then it's 11:30 outside Sloane Square tube station. We're going for a few drinks on the World's End estate. Millwall will be coming straight down the Kings Road so we can come straight out of the estate

27

and steam right into 'em. Neither them nor the Old Bill will know what's hit 'em!"

"Sounds like it'll be a busy day, should be good." Kevin tried to sound enthusiastic. He didn't mind the rucking, but he was still worried about what Lee would get up to. "What's the plan for the England match in Munich?"

"All I need to know is that I can rely on you - you're my right hand man. If you're in, there's no ducking out if the going gets tough."

No danger of that, thought Kev. He hated Germans and they deserved the beating they were going to get. Whether they would be prepared for Lee was something else though.

"We'll be joining up with Arsenal, Millwall and Birmingham when we get out there," Lee continued, "so we don't want any bottlers with us. Know what I mean, Kev?" Lee wanted to make sure his mate would be with him all the way on this trip.

"Yeah, no worries, Lee. I'll be up for it."

"Good lad."

Sharon knocked and came into the room with a tray of coffees and biscuits. Lee didn't even look up.

"What are you two plottin'?"

"Nothing you need to worry about, Shaz." Lee patted her stocking clad thigh as she sat down. "So I can count on you on Saturday?"

"Yep," said Kev as he dipped a chocolate biscuit into his mug of coffee.

"I'll confirm all the flight details and cost for Germany once I've got definite numbers."

"So you're not wanting the cash up front?"

"Nah, just gonna put it all on plastic. So as long as I get the cash from everyone before the bill comes in I'll be covered."

"Excellent! Who else is a definite?"

"Usual mob - Terry, Mike, John an' Ian. There's a few others wanting to join us."

"Yeah, like who?"

"There's some mates of Ian from Woolwich that want to join in. They've been to a few Chelsea matches with us before."

"Were they the ones at West Ham with us?"

"Yeah. And there's a geezer called Joe who's wanting to join the firm too."

"Who?"

"That's what I said when Ian mentioned 'im. He's been coming to Chelsea for a while now and heard we were a good firm. So apparently he's been asking around about joining us. That's how Ian got to know 'im. Ian says he's pretty game so I told him to see if this Joe lad wanted to come to the Manchester game with us."

"And? Is he?"

"Dunno, Ian gave 'im the details in case he decided to come along. All I can say is that if he wants in on the firm he'll be there, if not he can forget it!"

"Well, we'll 'ave to wait and see, eh?"

"Yep. Anyway, I've got some other business to attend to this afternoon." He ran his had up Sharon's thigh and under the hemline of her skirt. "Gotta keep Lolita satisfied!" Lee added, winking at Kevin.

Sharon put her arms around Lee and grinned. "Cheeky!"

Lee pulled Sharon up and began to push her towards the bedroom.

"I'll see you two later," said Kevin as he followed the pair out of the living room, but headed in the opposite direction. When there was no reply he looked back to see Lee lifting Sharon's top to get to her large breasts. He quietly closed the front door and walked down the street.

"Fuck Millwall, fuck England," he muttered as the cold Autumn wind cut right through his Duffer jacket.

"You shouldn't be so nasty to him," Sharon said to Lee as she lay beside him on the bed. "He's worried that things are getting out of control. So am I, come to that."

"Look, Shaz, it ain't just me. Everyone is getting pissed off with him and they're all having a pop at me about it cos he's my mate. He's gotta realise he's in the big league now. Anyway, I'm sure there's plenty of other things we could be doing rather than talking about Kevin." Lee ran his hand down Sharon's naked body and pushed his fingers into her moist pussy.

She parted her stocking clad legs (Lee always wanted her to leave them on) and moaned. "Oh Lee, give it to me."

"Don't worry, darlin', I will. But not just yet, I want some fun first!" Lee turned her around until she was on all fours.

Why couldn't it be like this all the time, she thought as Lee's throbbing cock pounded in and out of her as she approached orgasm.

CHAPTER FIVE

It was only Tuesday and Kevin was already starting to dread Saturday. He couldn't think straight or concentrate on his work at all. *What could he or Sharon do to calm Lee down?*

"Bollocks!"

He straightened up, ran his fingers through his short dark hair, and tried to continue with the consumer research report he had in front of him. The phone broke his unsteady concentration.

"Good morning, Kevin Murray speaking."

"Good morning, Kevin Murray speaking, this is Lee Jones speaking . . . "

"Yo, Lee, how's it going?"

"Talk about sounding posh for a South Londoner, Kev!"

"Gotta keep up appearances y'know. Keep the bosses impressed, the customers happy!"

"Yeah, know what y'mean. Anyway, on to more important things. Looks like everyone is turning out on Saturday."

"Excellent! How many do y'reckon?"

"Dunno. Hundreds. Enough to teach those Millwall cunts a thing or two!"

"Sounds good to me."

"Knew I could count on you, Kev."

"Not that old record again, Lee!" Kevin was sick and tired of hearing about his lack of commitment to the firm.

"Sorry, mate."

"Listen, you ain't got anything to worry about. I'll be there. Wild horses couldn't keep me away!"

"What about a wild whore?"

"Not even a wild whore!"

They both laughed.

"Better get going, Lee. Boss on the loose!"

"No problems, see ya Saturday."

"Yeah, see ya."

Kevin put the phone down and buried his head back into the report. If nothing else, a good ruck on Saturday would help him get rid of some of the work stress that had built up over the last few weeks.

The Millwall fans streamed out of the carriages onto the platform at Sloane Square tube station. The heaving crowd surged up the steps and through the police who were taken by surprise by the sheer weight of numbers. The Millwall boys poured out onto the street and started to swagger down the Kings Road into enemy territory.

The Saturday shoppers watched in silence as 400 pairs of designer trainers and label jackets sauntered past. Mad Mike was watching too as he punched a phone number into his portable phone.

"Lee? It's Mike."

"Mike? Great, can you see them yet?"

"See them? Can't you hear them?" He held the phone out towards the now chanting mob. "There's fuckin' hundreds of them, Lee!"

"Right, we're on our way."

Lee tucked his own mobile phone into his inside jacket pocket and addressed a pub full of Chelsea hooligans. "Right, that's it lads. They're on our manor and coming this way, and there's fuckin' hundreds of them!"

Drinks were finished in one gulp, and the adrenaline started pumping as everyone made for the pub's doors. Even Kevin felt the excitement that came from the promise of a ruck, but he still dreaded Lee's actions.

Lee looked every bit the general as he led his army onto the Kings Road to meet the oncoming Millwall. Chelsea were pouring out of pubs from all directions, and the two mobs began to quicken their pace as they caught sight of each other. A mixture of sheer excitement and terror urged them forward.

The adrenaline pounded as the first blows were thrown. The police were hopelessly outnumbered and had to stand by and watch while they waited for back-up. Shouts of threats and warnings filled the air as the two mobs merged and commenced battle.

"Come on you Millwall cunts!" Lee lunged at his first victim, smacking him square in the jaw. The pleasure rushed through his body as he set to work on his prey. All around him, arms and legs were lashing out, and there was the occasional flash of steel.

Eventually, the police were ready to move in, this time with dogs and horses. The fighting broke up a little, but running battles continued all the way down the Kings Road until the police had swamped the area. The hooligan's common enemy had come out on top again.

"Fuckin' scum! They always spoil our fun!" Lee remarked as some of his firm made their way through the side streets towards Fulham Road and Stamford Bridge. The mob muttered their agreement.

"I see you were back on form, Kev," Lee said to his mate who was walking beside him. "I'm proud of you." He patted Kevin on the back.

Kevin smiled. He was pleased with the way he had floored a couple of Millwall mugs before being chased away by the police dogs.

NO-ONE LIKES US,
NO-ONE LIKES US,
NO-ONE LIKES US - WE DON'T CARE!
WE ARE MILLWALL,
SUPER MILLWALL,
WE ARE MILLWALL FROM THE DEN!

The famous battle cry echoed around Chelsea's huge West Stand, creating one of the heaviest atmospheres Lee had ever experienced at Stamford Bridge. He was torn between admiration for the visitors' show of strength, in what was after all the Chelsea end, and his urge to do something about it.

"There's fuckin' hundreds of the bastards in here!" he yelled out to his firm.

Everyone was too busy picking out some of the infiltrators in the crowd to bother with the action on the pitch.

"C'mon, Lee, there's some of the mugs!" It was John, back from a scouting trip, and he pointed out some lads wearing Junior Gaultier leather jackets and Stone Island jeans. "Let's fuckin' have the cunts!"

"Oi! John! Cool it, they're just jailbait!" Lee cautioned, not wanting to kick things off too early and risk missing the main Millwall contingent.

"Leave it out Lee! They're taking the piss! Let's do it!"

"Look, wait until there's a goal or something and then we'll go in. Now, go and get the rest of them so we can firm up properly."

John nodded and moved off into the crowd. Kevin just looked on with mixed feelings.

Chelsea were on the attack. The home support in the West Stand were up on their feet, roaring their team on. Even Lee's mob were watching intently now as they urged the Blues on. The cheers and shouts were deafening as the ball hit the back of the Millwall net and the Chelsea fans jumped up and down.

FLYING HIGH UP IN THE SKY,
WE'LL KEEP THE BLUE FLAG FLYING HIGH,
FROM STAMFORD BRIDGE TO WEMBLEY,
WE'LL KEEP THE BLUE FLAG FLYING HIGH!

The celebrations seemed to go on for ages. For Lee and the firm, however, it was the signal for the real fireworks to begin. A blue coloured flare was fired into a group of taunting Millwall casuals a few rows ahead of them, and Lee and his mob stormed over the seats, heading in the same direction.

Lee lashed out at the nearest Millwall fan, letting his Stanley do all the work. Slicing the lad's face from ear to mouth was easy work. All around there was chaos as the rival fans steamed in.

Kevin was pounding a Millwall fan as he looked up to see Lee pouncing on another victim with his knife. Kevin belted his victim in anger and dropped him to the ground, but his attention was drawn towards Lee, lashing out time and time again. He shook his head as he backed off slightly, but that moment's hesitation earned him a punch in the mouth. All he saw was a gold fingered fist flash past his face.

"Shit!" He spun around and retaliated with both fists. Eventually, to Kevin's relief, the fighting started to ebb and was brought under control when the police moved into the stand.

Lee and Mike watched the police sort out the Millwall fans.

"They'll never get us!" Mike said, his voice buzzing with the trouble.

"The coppers or Millwall?"

They laughed as some of the others came into sight.

"Oi, Kev, what happened to you?" Lee asked as his friend approached.

Kevin was wiping some blood from his cheek where the ring had caught his skin. "Some Millwall mug tried to act the smart cunt, so I done the bastard."

"Good lad! Glad to see you ain't lost your bottle mate." Lee glared at the others to see if anyone would doubt him or Kevin now. Nobody did.

The jubilant crowd streamed out of Stamford Bridge into the Fulham Road, and among them was Lee's mob, inconspicuous as they made their way to Fulham Broadway tube station.

Lee looked around him. There was no point in hanging around, waiting for the Millwall to come out. *It's like a bloody police state*, he thought. "Kev! Make sure everyone knows it's London Bridge now!"

"Calm down Lee, everyone knows! Why can't we just leave it? We got a result today and London Bridge ain't our manor."

"No one is making you go, mate. Besides I thought you hadn't lost your bottle? Don't panic, Kev, it'll be over in seconds." He looked questioningly at Kevin who just looked away. "Look, if you can't handle playing in the big league go and watch Fulham or something!"

"I'm coming, okay!"

"Okay, just make sure you keep the form you've been using this afternoon," Lee added as they squeezed onto the packed tube train.

At London Bridge, the Chelsea firm immediately split into smaller groups and waited on various parts of the concourse.

"How many do you reckon, Lee? About a hundred?"

"You could be right, Mike. It'll be more than enough cos we ain't gonna be running anywhere. Where's John and Terry?"

"They're watching the tube." It was Kevin who replied, touching the tender place on his cheek. "That bastard's gone an' marked my face!"

"Aw, gorgeous!" Mike said, as he grabbed hold of Kevin and pretended to kiss his cheek.

"Fuck off, Mike!"

"Boys, boys! Calm down." Lee smiled to himself. Everything was in place. Millwall were about to be Bushwacked.

Then Lee's phone rang. "John?"

"Yeah, the train's just arrived and they're about to get off."

"You two, get down here!" Lee said to Kevin and Mike as the phone went back into his jacket. Then he spoke to the others standing around him. "Right lads, firm up! We'll have 'em at the entrance!"

Kevin sighed. Years ago, they used to put the heads of traitors on London Bridge. If Lee had his way, history would be repeating itself.

The Millwall firm swaggered up the steps from the tube, smug at the thought of giving Chelsea the slip. They were all too busy boasting to notice the gang of lads watching them from the main station.

A bottle crashed in the middle of them.

"Ambush!"

Someone sussed it straight off and they started to look about. By then, Lee and the other Chelsea boys were running at them, chanting, CHELSEA!

Lee's heart pounded faster and faster as he rushed to front the Millwall mob. He lashed out at one of them with his blade. The knife ripped through the youth's arm as he held it up to protect his face against the glinting steel.

Mike crashed a metal rubbish bin across a lad's head and the Millwall fan fell to the ground unconscious. Lee looked for someone else to attack, but most of the Millwall supporters had disappeared, leaving a few die-hards to stand and fight.

While the rest of the firm were chasing the remnants of the fleeing Millwall into the underground, Lee spotted one of them trying to crawl away. He nudged Mike and they sneaked up on him. Kevin got there first though, and kicked him up the arse and laughed as the lad turned in horror. As he started to look around, more Chelsea had gathered, all grinning and blocking off any escape route. His panic stricken face disappeared under a sea of kicking trainers. This was one sport that was not advertised in the Adidas catalogue.

Kevin started to move back as the attack became more frenzied, and he watched the whole incident with mixed feelings; part of him wanting to join in and part of him wanting to walk away. It started off all right, but now they were out to kill someone and he didn't want to be a part of it. He was so wound up in his own thoughts that he didn't notice the coppers coming up behind him, and the next thing he knew he was being manhandled into a waiting van.

CHAPTER SIX

Kevin sat in the police cell with his head in his hands. *Why me? Why not Lee or any of the others? Surely the Old Bill saw Lee attacking that Millwall boy with his blade? They can't be that blind?*

Footsteps and voices outside the cell door made him look up. His muscles tensed and his face hardened in readiness to hurl abuse at the copper bastards on the other side of the heavy metal door.

The sound of keys in locks was followed by the door opening. DI Welsh took one step into the cell and looked down at the Chelsea casual. "Well, well, Kevin, I hear you haven't been behaving yourself."

"What's it to you?"

"Now, now, there's no need to be like that. I just want you to answer a few questions. There's a few things on my mind that are bothering me."

"I've got nothin' to say to you!"

"We'll soon see about that, won't we." Welsh turned and walked out of the cell and then indicated for Kevin to follow him.

But Kevin stayed where he was. "I told you, I ain't got nothin' to say!"

"Come on, Kevin, this won't hurt."

"You don't frighten me!"

Welsh smirked and nodded to two waiting constables. They came into the cell and grabbed Kevin. He stood up and shook them off, and then headed out of the cell.

"Coffee, Kevin?"

He shook his head.

"Tea then?"

"No."

"Cigarette?"

"No! I don't want nothin' from you!" Kevin sat back in the plastic chair and folded his arms. He looked around the room, and thought that nothing had changed since his visit to the interview room the last time they had hauled him in for football violence. Still the same old drab paintwork, the hideous floor tiles and a copper at the door, standing like a tailor's dummy.

"Well, I'm sure you won't mind if I do." Welsh lit a cigarette and blew the smoke in Kevin's direction.

Kevin just turned away.

Welsh grinned and switched on the tape recorder. "This interview is being recorded. This is DI Jim Welsh. Present in the room is Detective Sergeant MacKenzie and the interviewee Kevin Murray. The time is 21:44. Kevin, I'm going to ask you some questions regarding a disturbance this evening at London Bridge station at which you were arrested. You have been made aware of your rights. Do you still waive your right to a brief?"

"Yeah, fire away. I ain't got anything to hide."

"Now, tell me, why were you at London Bridge station?"

"I was going for the tube."

"Who was with you?"

"No one."

"Did you see anyone you knew at the station?"

"No."

"Are you sure?"

"Yeah."

41

"Do you know Lee Jones?"

"Yeah."

"And you didn't see Jones at the station?"

"No. I just told you that I didn't see anyone I knew."

"I just want to be sure," said Welsh before sipping from a coffee mug, "because I know for a fact that Jones was at the station with a large group - some of whom you know too."

"Yeah, like who?"

"John Howden, Mike Hunter, Terry Johnston, Ian Smith, Rob Wilson - to name but a few."

"Well, I never seen 'em," Kevin said, going through the usual questions and answers routine with the plods.

"But they were there and so where you. Now, I think that you were part of this group and I think that you were involved in the disturbance that they created."

"Yeah, well, you think wrong."

"I don't think so. I also think that this group of well known Chelsea fans were initially loitering with intent because London Bridge station is used by Millwall fans. I think that this group of Chelsea fans were waiting for the Millwall fans, waiting to ambush them. The Millwall fans duly arrived and the Chelsea fans then attacked them, causing the disturbance to which we were called. What do you think?"

"I didn't know anything about it. I was on my own. I told you."

"I'll tell you something else," Welsh continued. "I think your friend Jones organised this ambush as well as organising the trouble in the West Stand at Stamford Bridge today."

"Nah, Lee ain't into that kinda thing."

"I know for a fact that Jones is well known as an instigator of trouble involving Chelsea fans."

"I told you, Lee doesn't get involved in that kinda stuff."

"And neither do you, I take it?"

"Yeah, that's right," Kevin said, looking Welsh straight in the eye. "I don't."

"Then why were you seen and picked up fleeing from the scene of the crime?"

"I was trying to get away from the trouble. I had nothing to do with it."

"Then how did you come by that mark on your face?" Welsh asked in a tone that suggested he knew the answer anyway.

"Knocked it on a cupboard door this morning."

"Is that right?"

"Yeah." Kevin was getting a bit worried. He couldn't understand how this Welsh geezer knew so much. He couldn't decide if Welsh was bluffing or not.

"Fine. Back to tonight. Are you trying to tell me that you walked through a crowd of people you knew and didn't try to help them or try to stop the fighting?"

"What? Stop a mob of a hundred blokes armed with blades and the like? It would be impossible! As for helping out, I told you I ain't into that kinda thing."

"Blades? How did you know there were knives involved?"

Kevin's heart sank. *Shit! Can't let anything else slip. Keep cool.* "I saw a couple of blokes with them, that's all."

"Did you recognise them?"

"Nope."

"Could you describe them?"

43

"Listen, I wasn't wanting to get involved so I didn't stop to take in the view."

"You and Jones go back a long way, don't you?" said Welsh, changing tact.

"Yeah, so?"

"So, how comes you don't know the kind of thing that he's arranging? If he's a good friend, if not a close friend, I'm surprised he doesn't tell you."

"Lee's like me, he ain't into trouble and stuff like that. Anyway, we don't tell each other everything."

"Oh, you don't? What about his girlfriend, what's her name?" Welsh looked through the file in front of him. "Ah, yes, Miss Sharon Gillespie. Now, she must be close to him and you must know her pretty well too."

"You leave Sharon out of this!" exploded Kevin.

Welsh realised that he'd found a soft spot in Murray's mental armour.

Kevin felt a bit edgy after his burst of anger, especially now that Welsh had brought Sharon into it all.

"Yes, Miss Gillespie, what does she think about her boyfriend's antics?"

"As I keep tellin' you, Lee ain't into anything."

"Well, you said yourself that you don't tell each other everything. Maybe Jones tells his girlfriend instead?"

"No way, Sharon hates anything to do with violence!"

"What about drugs?"

"Drugs? What's drugs got to do with it?"

"Just let me ask the questions. Yes, drugs. What does Sharon think about drugs? In fact, is she a drug user herself?"

"Sharon? Never! She hates drugs and drug users!"

"You seem to know a lot about what Sharon thinks. You two a bit friendly? Maybe she's getting scared of Jones and she's turning to you . . . as a friend of course."

"Don't be daft."

"Well then, I'm sure Sharon will be able to answer a few of these questions and confirm what you've said."

"Don't you fuckin' bother bringing her in! She doesn't know anything!"

"Knows anything about what, Kevin?"

Shit! It's getting too hot for comfort. Don't let this Welsh cunt get to you. "I mean she and Lee just go out together an' that. Sharon doesn't like football so Lee never talks to her about it."

"So what do they talk about?"

"How should I know? I'm not stuck to Lee."

"Well that's something else I can ask her myself then."

Bastard! He's blackmailing me into grassing! "I told you, Sharon doesn't know anything. Lee doesn't know anything and I don't know anything. What do you expect me to say?"

"I'm just wanting some information about a gang of violent Chelsea fans who are terrifying the life out of ordinary fans and the general public. Not to mention a gang of Chelsea fans who are supplying Ecstasy to ravers."

"Well, I don't know nothin' about any of that either. So why am I still here?"

"I was hoping you'd be able to give me some information and I still think you can."

45

"I told you, I don't know anything! Listen, I'm gettin' sick of this, I want my brief!"

Welsh glared at him. He knew Kevin had the answers to his questions. "Right, this interview has been terminated. The time is 22:32."

Welsh switched off the tape recorder and finished his cold coffee. "Kevin, you're not being silly are you? Withholding information from me?"

Kevin stayed silent, his heart beating somewhere in his throat.

"I thought you were better than the rest. I thought you had a little more sense than to keep quiet."

Kevin just stared back at Welsh.

"Well, if you change your mind you know where I am." Welsh stood up and headed for the door. Before he opened it he turned back. "Think about it, Kevin. Be a good lad, eh?" He then opened the door and disappeared down the hallway.

The tailor's dummy nodded to Kevin who stood up and walked to the door.

Kevin sat in his cell waiting for his brief, his back against the wall and his arms resting on top of his pulled up knees. His mind churned over and over, thinking about what had happened. *That bastard expected me to grass on my best mate! Never! Mind you, it would be one way to get Lee to cool off. No, no! That's not the way to do it! What would happen if anyone found out I had grassed! I'd be killed! But who would know? How would they find out?*

He shook his head to bring an end to all the questions, but it didn't work. They still spun around his head. He knew he couldn't grass on his mate. It would

46

be one way to straighten Lee out, but he had to find another way to do it.

He heard the door being unlocked and he looked up. His brief popped his head in. "Right, Mr Murray, you're out of here."

"Thank God for that!"

"Yes, well, they haven't charged you and by the sounds of it, you've not said anything incriminating. So, you're free to go."

"Great! Thanks, Mr Hutchinson! I owe you one."

"No problem. Now, can I give you a lift anywhere?"

"Yeah, if you're heading Streatham way."

"I'm not going that far, but I'll drop you at the station."

"That'll be great, yeah."

Kevin's walk changed into a swagger as he passed Welsh and grinned at him.

"Remember what I said, Kevin. Hope to see you soon."

Kevin turned and stuck his middle finger in the air, and then backed through the door.

CHAPTER SEVEN

While sauntering along Fulham Road to the pub, Kevin felt pleased with his performance at the police station the previous night. It would definitely make Lee trust him again, especially where his honour was concerned. Kevin smiled to himself as he neared the pub. *I hope that bastard Terry is in tonight. My news will soon shut him up!* Kevin couldn't wait and he quickened his pace until he reached his destination, then he coolly swaggered into the pub.

"Yo Kev! How ya doin'?"

"Alright Lee!" Kevin said before shouting across to the barman. "Bottle of Sol, mate."

"What happened to you last night, then?" It was Terry, ready to have a dig at Kevin.

"Yeah, Kev, what happened? One minute you were beside me, next minute I saw you getting bundled into a police van! I can't understand how none of us were lifted."

"I dunno cos I didn't get charged with anything. I was just picked up. I don't think they could have seen me laying into those Millwall mugs. They didn't say anything about that."

"So what did they want, then?" Terry was wanting to try and nail Kevin so Lee would turn against him.

"Some git called Welsh, DI I think, was asking questions about you Lee," Kev said, totally ignoring Terry.

"Yeah? What was he wanting to know?"

"Wanted to know about the ruck last night and if you arranged it and if you arranged any of the trouble in the West Stand."

"So what did you say?"

"Hope you never grassed any of us, Kev!" Terry said, butting in.

"Shut up, Tel, and let 'im finish!"

"Never said a word! I couldn't make out if he was fishing or if he's been watching us lot for a while."

"What do you mean - 'us'?" another voice said.

"John, he reeled off nearly everyone's name and he knew about the Ecstasy. It was a nightmare. Still kept quiet though. He's a real bastard."

"So, we're wanted men, eh!" Lee had a grin from ear to ear that would have put a Cheshire cat to shame.

"Wanted is about the right word. Another thing, you'll never guess how Welsh tried to make me talk. He brought Sharon into the conversation."

"What!" Lee's grin turned into fury. "Why?"

"He said if I didn't grass, then he'd get Sharon into the station. I still kept quiet and I managed to get 'im off Sharon."

"Well done," Lee said appreciatively. "I don't want Shaz brought into any of this."

"But why bring her into it anyway? She's got nothin' to do with you, Kev." It sounded as though Terry was trying to save face with Lee, but it wasn't working.

Lee was impressed with Kevin, and the way he'd kept his nerve with the Old Bill. "You trying to tell me you wouldn't try and protect Sharon?"

"Didn't say that, Lee," Terry said quietly.

"Just as well, cos I'd fuckin' do ya if you landed my girlfriend in this!"

49

Terry looked nervously down, not wanting to get on the bad side of Lee.

"Sounds as though you've done a good job, Kev," Lee added.

"I just hope the Old Bill don't come sniffin' 'round us!" Terry just didn't know when to leave well alone.

"Terry, will you shut it!" shouted Lee. "Kev did a good job! I doubt if you could've handled it any better!"

Terry felt embarrassed and turned to talk to John.

"Kev, the Old Bill won't pick Shaz up, will they?"

"Nah, no way, Lee. Honest."

"Good, I hope not."

Kevin looked around to see who else was in to hear what had happened. Everyone had heard his story, but now they were all laughing about the ruck. Except Mike who was too engrossed in the fruit machine.

Kevin leaned against the bar behind Lee and joined in the conversation. Same old Sunday chat, comparing notes on who smacked who, what the other mob were wearing . . .

The last orders bell sounded.

"Another beer, Kev?" Lee asked.

"Nah."

"How come?"

Kevin finished his drink. "I'm shattered, can't remember what time I got out the cells, and I've got an early start tomorrow."

"Okay, I'll phone you during the week. I think I've managed a lock-in tonight for us."

"Enjoy yourself then. See ya."

"Yeah, see ya!"

The rest of the mob nodded their farewells as Kevin headed for the door and for home.

Kevin threw his Duffer jacket onto the settee and sat down beside it. He propped his Puma States on the coffee table and closed his eyes. Before he knew it he was drifting off to sleep, but he jumped awake when his door buzzer sounded.

He went to the hall and picked up the intercom. "Hello?"

"Oh Kev, I'm glad you're in. It's Sharon."

"Hi, come on up." He pushed the door release and opened the front door. He could hear the scuff of her soles and the click of her heels as she made her way up the stairs. Her blonde hair appeared the flight below and he smiled.

"Hiya!"

"Hi! I'll never get used to those stairs!"

She sounded breathless and he laughed. He closed the door and ushered Sharon into the living room.

"To what do I owe this pleasure?"

Sharon sat down on the settee and crossed her shapely legs. "It's Lee."

"What about 'im?"

Kevin moved his jacket to another seat and sat beside her. He could smell the Chanel perfume she always wore - the perfume that always drove him wild.

"I don't think I can take much more! He's gonna do something really bad and get caught for it and I can't do anything to stop 'im!" She bowed her head and tried to stop the tears but it didn't work. They flowed down her cheeks and her body shook with emotion.

Kevin put his arm around her shoulders. "It's okay, Sharon, I understand."

"Oh, Kev!" Her head landed on his chest and she sobbed even more.

Kevin put his other arm around her and held her.

"You're the only one who understands and feels the same as me," she said between sobs.

"Shhh, it's okay. I'm sure we'll think of something."

He could feel her body shaking as she cried, and he held her tighter. "Sharon, everything will be okay."

"I hope so."

"Do you want something to drink? Coffee or something stronger?"

"Coffee will be fine, thanks. I'll go and sort my face."

"And here's me thinking that you didn't wear make-up!"

She laughed a little, and cheered up slightly.

Kevin felt sorry for her; she looked so lost and helpless. He looked down at her tear-streaked face and kissed her cheek. "Everything will work out fine, you'll see."

She put her hand to the side of his face and ran her fingers through his short dark hair. "With you here, I'm sure everything will be."

She pulled his head down to hers and kissed him, this time on the lips. He responded and put his arms around her again. Their tongues met and they both started to get tingling sensations through their bodies. He pulled her closer as the kiss became more intense.

Kevin realised what he was doing. He was kissing his best mate's girlfriend! He pulled away.

"Kevin, what's wrong?"

"This isn't right. I shouldn't have taken advantage when you're so cut up about Lee."

"Kevin, to be honest with you, I don't think me and Lee are going to last much longer."

"Sharon, that's not the point. If he found out, you know what would happen."

"Sorry."

"It's my fault." He couldn't resist kissing the top of her head. "I'll get the coffee."

"And I'll sort my face!"

"I'm sorry about earlier, Kev," Sharon said as he brought two steaming hot mugs of coffee through from the kitchen.

"It's my fault, I shouldn't have done it when you were so upset."

"Not about that silly!" She patted his thigh. "About crying."

"It's okay, honest," he said, taking her hand in his.

"I just don't know what to do anymore. I hardly see Lee these day's y'know. I don't even know what he's thinking now. We're drifting apart, that's why I think that we're not going to last much longer. But when I see him, all the doubt and worry disappears. And then when I'm alone it all creeps back again."

"Have you seen him today?"

Sharon shook her head.

"So you won't know about last night then?"

"No. Why, what happened?"

She snuggled in a bit closer to him and moved her hand further across his thigh while Kevin launched into a description of the previous night, including getting picked up . . .

When Kevin woke up, the early morning light was pouring through the living room window and he was lying along the settee with Sharon in his arms. He checked his watch. Six o'clock. *Shit, work. Shit, Lee. What if he went around to see Sharon after the pub?*

"Sharon? Sharon?"

She stirred slightly.

"Sharon, wake up, it's six o'clock."

"Mmm, what was that, what time is it?"

"Six o'clock, I'll phone a taxi for you."

Sharon opened her eyes. "Good morning, Kevin."

As Kevin moved to get up, Sharon kissed him and he her kissed back. Her slender arms then pulled him back down. Their tongues once again met and entwined themselves. Sharon ran her fingers up and down Kevin's back and slowly eased his Boss shirt out from his jeans.

"Sharon."

"Yes?"

"What are you doing?"

"Nothing," she replied, her hands exploring beneath his shirt.

"That's okay then."

Her fingers gently caressed his muscular back. Kevin moaned as his groin awoke with pleasure. Sharon had moved her hands to his chest and were undoing his shirt, but he made it easier by leaning up slightly and taking it off. Her eyes looked his body up and down and smiled.

Kevin leaned on one elbow and he ran his other hand down her full breasts and flat stomach. Sharon closed her eyes slightly and sighed. Her breasts heaved and

54

his manhood got bigger. Between them they managed to undress and caress each other on the settee.

Their bodies worked together and their hearts pounded faster and faster. Eventually Kevin eased his aching cock into Sharon's warm and wet love tunnel. She sighed again.

Kevin moved slowly at first, seeing how much Sharon's face lit up. He licked her erect nipples as he moved up and down.

"Kevin, you tease!"

He thrusted harder and harder. Sharon clutched his backside until they both reached a climax. He shot his load and she almost screamed in ecstasy. Their sweating bodies slid beside each other as they lay back, breathless.

"Where do we go from here then, Sharon?" Kev asked, as they lay in each other's arms.

"To the shower - we've both got to get to work."

"You know what I mean."

"Oh, him. How's he gonna find out? Are you gonna tell 'im, cos I ain't."

"I'm telling no one."

"Good, let's shower."

"Ladies first."

"Oh, aren't you joining me?" Sharon asked, her voice full of promise.

Kevin smiled and pulled her off the settee and towards the bathroom. The shower was as pleasing as the settee as they made love for a second time.

CHAPTER EIGHT

Nine o'clock on Saturday morning and Euston station looked like a designer label fashion sale. Lee's chest swelled with pride as he looked around. "This is a fuckin' magic firm, Kev. There must be at least 300 here."

Kevin nodded in agreement. Even he was getting worked up about the day ahead. He knew they would take Manchester apart with this mob.

"Everyone is well turned out too," Lee continued. "Armani, Stone Island, Duffer, you name it, it's here."

"Yeah, Lee, we'll show those Manc scum how to dress. Joe Bloggs ain't really Premier League material!"

The two of them nodded to the known faces as the crowd gathered together and slowly made its swaggering way onto the platform for the Manchester train.

* * *

High up in Euston's police room, DI Welsh surveyed the scene below with a look of disdain. "Sergeant! Get in touch with Manchester and give them a warning. This little lot will rip them apart if they get the chance."

"Yes, Guv."

"Also, Sergeant, what about that FIU plain clothes officer. Is he down there?"

"Yes, he's settled in well. He's already on speaking terms with the top boys."

"What? Jones as well?"

"Yes, Guv. After that request we put in for assistance, he's starting to hang around with Jones's firm."

"Excellent. I can feel Jones coming into our clutches at last."

* * *

Joe Francis had been in the Met for a few years now. He had wanted to join the army, but his parents and girlfriend had talked him out of it and into joining the police force. Cadet training was a breeze and he hoped to get in with the horses or dogs, but the powers that be decided his destiny was pounding the beat. Which was all right, but he wanted more of the action and asked for a stint in CID. He got in on a trial basis, impressed the DI, and was given the opportunity to join the Football Intelligence Unit. He wasn't too keen at first, but after all the bad press coverage the England supporters were getting all over Europe he wanted to help nail the ignorant bastards.

But it wasn't long before he discovered that the thugs weren't ignorant. The majority of them were office workers - from clerks right up to managers. Some had degrees, families and a good standard of living. There also wasn't one scruff among them! Getting involved with Chelsea had opened his eyes to the smart thinking and smart dressing of the hooligans that the media seemed to be blissfully unaware of.

Naturally, he was concerned in case any of the firm found out about him being both a copper and a grass. He had read the files on the previous operations that hadn't been successful, and he knew all about what happened to covert officers if the hooligan gangs found out they were Old Bill. Some of them were lucky and got away with a good kicking, but others weren't so lucky and ended up in intensive care with severe head injuries and stab wounds. It didn't help matters much with the recent showing of that TV documentary about police infiltrating a football firm. It just made everybody more suspicious of any new faces popping up.

* * *

Joe stopped in front of a shop window to check out his new outfit of Armani jeans, Stone Island jacket and Adidas Campus trainers. *Not bad, not bad at all! I could get used to this label dressing and the notoriety!*

He moved on towards the train station and looked around to check out the faces, and he couldn't believe the amount of labelled-up youths heading to the station. He shook his head and smiled to himself. His boss was having a tough time accepting that the types of lads the firms attracted were wearing such expensive clothes, and had expected Joe to make do with cheap jeans and DM boots! All his boss needed to do was to contact the nicks about town to discover what the hooligans were wearing, and he'd soon find out why Joe's expenses claims were so high.

He approached the station concourse and spotted Lee and the rest of the lads. "Oi! Lee, are we going first class, or what?"

"Sure are, Joe - we're Chelsea ain't we! Nothin' but the best! So stick with us, you'll learn a lot."

"Don't worry," said Joe, without a hint of sarcasm in his voice, "I'm picking everything up as I go along."

They made their way onto the platform and headed straight for the first class carriages, much to the dismay of the British Rail staff present who knew there was no way of stopping them without causing some aggravation.

Joe sat at a table with John and Mike. Lee sat beside Kevin at a table further down, not wanting to sit too close to the new boy before sussing him out a bit. "Kev, what do you think about Joe?" he said, making sure Joe was out of earshot.

"He seems okay and the word is that he's well game. How?"

"I don't know if I can trust him. He just came from nowhere and no one knows him or nothin'. Then the next thing y'know, he's around all the time. It's probably nothin' Kev, but you can't be too careful. Know what I mean?"

"Calm down, Lee, there's nothin' to worry about. Mike reckons he's okay and some blokes who drink down The Glasgow said he's game. We'll find out today if he is up to it or not. Now come on and get the cards out."

"Yeah, awright. Must be getting paranoid in my old age."

As long as you don't get paranoid about Sharon, thought Kevin.

"Good afternoon," said the muffled voice through the tannoy. "This is the Intercity London Euston to Manchester. We will be arriving in Manchester in approximately ten minutes."

Lee stood up and moved from table to table giving his firm pep talks. "Right lads! Remember, the Old Bill will have their usual welcoming committee waiting for us, so keep cool, blend in and no singing. If United are about, let them come to us. We're on their patch so we don't need to go looking for it."

The adrenaline and drugs started to pump around the bodies in the carriage as the train pulled into the platform. The carriage doors whooshed open and the other passengers were pushed aside as the Chelsea firm disembarked.

"It's like a fuckin' army today!" Mike shouted to Lee.

"Yeah, good innit!"

"Yeah, brilliant, really buzzing."

A sharp push from a large police sergeant stopped them in their tracks. "Right lads, against the wall!"

The filth were everywhere. Dogs, horses, riot shields, the lot. All there to shepherd the Chelsea mob to Old Trafford.

A few lads tried to break away, but they soon retreated when they came face to face with the snarling German Shepherds.

So much for civil liberties thought Kevin, as a few of the boys started mouthing off at the police.

"C'mon lads, keep it quiet!" said Lee, not wanting to see anyone lifted by the police before anything had even happened. "Kev, keep your lot in line. This lot are jailbait just now."

"Right lads!" said someone with a Manchester accent.

They looked up to see a mounted police officer. "Hey! Look! It's a pig on horseback!" said Mike.

The mob laughed and the mounty looked around for a guilty looking suspect, but to no avail. "You're not in London now and you'll do exactly as you're told. You will receive an escort on foot to and from the ground. Anyone stepping out of line will be spending a lot longer than they planned up here. Let's go! Move!"

The procession started to walk down the ramp from the station onto the road, and immediately came across Manchester's Red Army.

"Oi, Lee! That's their firm coming out of that boozer," said an excited voice. "Let's go for it!"

"Cool it, Tel. It's jailbait. Let them come to us!"

The Manchester lads were walking parallel to the Chelsea mob on the opposite side of the street.

"It's gonna go soon, Lee," said Kev, feeling the buzz rising in his stomach.

"Keep cool, Kev, mate."

The Red Army were moving into the middle of the road. The police were so busy watching the Londoners that they seemed unaware of the other mob's movements.

SMASH!

Bottles started crashing around the Chelsea mob.

"Come on you Cockney cunts!"

"Think you're hard, Chelsea, c'mon then!"

The taunts and the sound of glass breaking eventually became too much for Lee. "C'mon Chelsea, let's fuckin' do it!"

They charged through the police escort and waded straight into the United fans. As Lee punched his enemy to the ground, he looked up and smiled. Small battles were breaking out all over the street, and the police were struggling to contain them all. He noticed

Kevin cracking his victim's head on a lamppost. He then turned back to find a brave Manc facing up to him. "Let's see what you're made of you Red bastard!"

Lee pounced like a wild cat and the lad fell to the ground under an array of punches and kicks. His opponent didn't put up much of a defence as Lee pounded the body under his knees, blood seeping to the pavement as the United hooligan's broken nose oozed the red stuff.

The Man United mob started to take to their heels with the police and Chelsea in pursuit. Mounted police reinforcements arrived and the rival factions were gradually separated with most of the arrests being from the Chelsea firm. The mounties pushed their horses against the fans, forcing them against shop windows.

The crackling of a megaphone came into life. "RIGHT YOU SMART ARSED COCKNEYS, ONE MORE BIT OF TROUBLE FROM YOU AND YOU'RE ALL . . . "

Lee started to hum the theme tune from *Z Cars*, and the rest of the firm joined in to drown out the crackling voice in mid sentence.

"SHUT IT! OR YOU'RE ALL NICKED!"

"Ah, fuck off, you Northern cunt!"

"WHAT SMART ARSE SAID THAT?"

"C'mon, do the Ol' Bill!" someone shouted as a bottle bounced off a mounty's helmet and the Chelsea charged.

The police backed off and Chelsea kept charging. As the missiles started to rain in on them, the Old Bill withdrew completely, leaving the Chelsea fans to run riot. The sound of breaking glass and car alarms was like music to Lee's ears.

Down a side street a small group of United fans emerged from a pub, seemingly unaware of the raucous in the main street.

"C'mon lads, down here!" Lee shouted, as he led his firm down the street after the unsuspecting group. They turned around at the noise of running footsteps, but it was too late to run.

Lee crashed his Adidas Shell Toe into the nearest fan's groin. Kevin followed suit, crashing his fist into another fan, and the rest of the mob set about their prey with equal veracity. Blades flashed and designer trainers found their targets as the Mancs clawed at the road in a futile attempt to escape the attack.

Kevin stopped to take a breath, totally knackered. *I'm getting too old for this,* he thought.

The Mancs were left flat out on the ground, struggling to cling to consciousness. It was difficult to tell whose blood was whose because all of the pools had merged into one. The fear that somebody would die ran through Kevin's mind as he watched Lee and the others continue to kick fuck out of the bodies on the deck. "Oi, Lee, they've 'ad enough."

"Fuckin' had enough? They're still breathing ain't they?"

"Shit man! C'mon, move it!" The Old Bill will be here in a minute and we're stuck in a dead end side street."

"Yeah, Kev's right, Lee. The coppers are all over the place it won't be long before they see us. Better leave these gits here." It was Joe who came to Kevin's defence.

"Fuck's sake!" Lee said, angry that his enjoyment was being cut short. "Right, let's go. When we get back onto the main road split into twos and threes and we'll all meet up at the ground."

When they got to the main road Lee grabbed Kevin. "Are you goin' soft? I was ready to finish 'em!"

"They had had enough, that's all."

"You're not turning into a sap?"

"Fuck off!"

"You better not be!"

"We won't always get away with it y'know," Kevin said, immediately realising that such reasoning was bound to fall on deaf ears.

"Give it a rest, we'll worry about that when it comes. Anyway, we'd better keep quiet. We don't want these northern bastards knowing where we're from."

CARE FREE, WHERE EVER YOU MAY BE, WE ARE THE FAMOUS CFC . . .

"Fuckin' great! One nil up with five minutes to go!" John had to shout to be heard.

"Look!" Terry pointed across the pitch as the police attempted to move to quell yet another disturbance. "It's all going off up in the seats!"

CHELSEA AGGRO! CHELSEA AGGRO!

Excellent, thought Lee, *this will stir the Mancs right up for after the match.*

"Oi!, Kev! Get everyone together and firm up at the main exit."

"Gotcha!" The excitement surged through his body again. *This is what it's all about, spontaneous violence with just fists and boots. None of this premeditated stuff, all Stanleys and razors.*

The final whistle interrupted Kevin's thoughts as the Chelsea fans reminded their hosts of the score. ONE NIL! ONE NIL!

The taunts directed towards the Stretford End were deafening. The response brought a smile to Kevin's face. YOU'LL NEVER MAKE THE STATION! YOU'LL NEVER MAKE THE STATION!

The PA system suddenly came to life. "WOULD ALL CHELSEA FANS PLEASE REMAIN IN THE GROUND AS THE EXIT GATES WILL NOT BE OPENED UNTIL THE AREA IS CLEAR OF CONGESTION. YOU WILL THEN BE ESCORTED TO THE TRAIN STATION."

"As if that'll stop us, eh, lads!"

Lee and the firm laughed and made their way to the gates so they would be the first out. As they neared the fence they could see coins and cans being tossed over by both set of fans. Numerous slanging matches were also taking place.

"See you at the station, ya Chelsea scum!"

"You'll never make it home alive!"

"Cockney slags!"

"London scum!"

But Chelsea gave as good as they got.

"You go down pub, you drink ten pints, get absolutely plastered, you go back 'ome and you beat your wife, you dirty northern bastards!"

SCUM! SCUM! SCUM! SCUM!

"Those bastards are getting a bit lippy for their own good!" said Lee. "Just 'cos we're penned in, they think they're brave!"

"Yeah, Lee, well out of order! C'mon do the gates. C'mon Chelsea do the gates!" Kevin screamed, lunging at the fence.

The mob swayed towards the already rocking fence and buckling gates. The police constables looked on in horror as hundreds of hooligans crushed onto the side of the pens. A few of the coppers were already radioing for assistance, and when the higher ranking officers saw what was happening they immediately ordered the gates to be unlocked. The ghost of Hillsborough still haunted them.

The Chelsea firm burst through and shoved past the police and straight into the Red Army. A flare was fired from the Chelsea mob into the tightly packed opposition, instantly scattering them in all directions. The air was thick with bricks and bottles as running battles filled the street.

A mounted police charge into the brawling mob was dangerous but highly effective. At the top of the street, the police managed to separate the mobs and direct the Chelsea fans towards Warwick Avenue railway station where a waiting train stood at the platform, ready to take the unruly fans into Manchester's Piccadilly. Before the train pulled away, all the carriages were stuffed full like cattle trucks.

The echoes of singing could be heard all through the station . . .   MAYBE IT'S BECAUSE I'M A LONDONER . . .

When they arrived at Piccadilly it was a like entering a police state. There was a solid line of police from the booking hall to the London platform, where another train waited for them.

"Fuckin' great this innit!" Lee said, obviously on a high. "Made everyone sit up and notice us today! Smile lads, we're on *Candid Camera*!"

The firm looked to where Lee was pointing and noticed press photographers straining over the police line.

"Well, let's give 'em what they want to see." Kevin stood in defiance and glared towards the cameras. It wasn't long before the rest of them joined in for the photo call.

Lee gloated and started singing again and everyone else joined in as they packed onto another dilapidated carriage. MAYBE IT'S BECAUSE I'M A LONDONER . . .

CHAPTER NINE

Kevin sat in silence as Lee and the others became more rowdy.

He felt a playful punch on his shoulder. "C'mon, Kev mate! Cheer up, we fuckin' won! On and off the pitch!" Lee's voice was slurred with the booze.

"Yeah, we did, didn't we. We done 'em good an' proper!" Kevin smiled at the thought of it.

"'Ere, Trace, get me an' me best mate a drink!" Lee shouted across to the shapely barmaid. "Look at those legs Kev, look at that arse! 'Ave you seen anythin' so raunchy in your life?"

"It's the size of her tits that get me!"

"Yeah, too fuckin' right!"

Tracy, on hearing what the lads had said, sauntered over slowly, swinging her assets. She placed the bottles of beer on the bar and leaned across, her breasts almost bursting out over her low cut lycra top. Lee and Kevin gulped in the view placed before them. "On the 'ouse, darlin'."

She looked playfully at Lee.

"Cheers, Trace. 'Ave one on me." Lee slid a crisp tenner into her swelling cleavage.

She leaned nearer Lee so her red lips were inches away from his right ear "I'm sure I will, lover boy."

Lee grinned at the ambiguous reply and turned to face her.

"I'll wait until after hours so I can relax over it more," she added.

Lee felt the excitement rush over him and his penis started to ache. "Yeah, well, you'll enjoy it more that way. Need some company?"

Tracy slowly ran her tongue across her lips. "Who do you have in mind, darlin'?"

"Why, me of course." He could feel his penis swell.

"Sounds good to me. I'll see you later, Lee." She blew a kiss at him and slowly turned away to carry on serving.

"What a fuckin' turn on! Can't wait! Did you see the way she moves!"

"Yeah, but what about Sharon?" asked Kevin. He didn't want her hurt anymore than he wanted Lee to find out what they had been getting up to behind his back.

"What about her? What she doesn't know won't hurt her. Anyway, that Tracy is beggin' for it. She can't wait for me to fuck 'er!"

"That's not the point! Sharon dotes on you, she's really hooked."

Not anymore she wasn't, but he wasn't going to be the one to tell Lee the news.

"Well, Tracy is hooked on me too my son, and I can't let her down, now can I?"

"Don't do it, Lee."

"Why? You gonna tell Shaz like?"

"Me? No way! What you do is your business, but I still think it's unfair to Sharon."

"You better not say anything, not to no one!"

"You can trust me. But can you trust the rest of them?"

He nodded over to the rest of the lads who were larking around. "They know better than to cross me."

69

The lads started to sing and Lee joined in, falling into line with the others.

Kevin shook his head. *Poor Sharon. Lee's loss but my gain!* Kevin thought. *If Lee didn't care, he damned well did.*

Kevin picked up his jacket, made signs that he was on his way, and looked over at Lee. "Are you going ahead with this?"

"Yeah, now fuck off home and don't breath a word to Shaz!"

"Yeah, yeah, see you later. Enjoy yourself."

Tracy appeared behind Lee and put her arms around him. "I will, don't you worry!" he grinned, slipping his arm around her and giving her a squeeze.

Tracy giggled and took a sip from a small bottle of vodka. "See ya, Kev, pity you couldn't join us. It could've been fun!"

Tracy blew a kiss at Kevin as he walked out the pub. Lee turned to her and kissed her. His tongue penetrated her mouth and his hands worked their way around to her voluptuous breasts.

"Not here," she said into Lee's ear.

"Where then?"

She jangled a set of keys. "They're for the flat above 'ere, an' it's empty . . . "

As soon as they entered the stark flat, they fell against a wall, kissing and groping each other. Tracy led him into a room, placed her coat on the floor and they lay down, Lee yanking his jacket off as he joined her.

Tracy's arms entwined themselves around Lee's neck as they kissed. His hand once again found her soft

70

breasts and hard nipples. His mouth moved from hers and made his way down her neck.

"Oh Lee . . . " Tracy sighed as he expertly brought a milky white breast out from under her top.

His tongue started to massage the erect nipple and Tracy started to moan. Her hands worked Lee's Armani shirt loose and she ran her painted nails up his back. Lee responded by shoving a knee in between her thighs and his right hand raised her mini skirt. Tracy parted her legs further and his hand found its way to her vagina. He smiled to himself because she wasn't wearing any panties.

Tracy unzipped Lee's jeans and his throbbing manhood came out. "Lee, fuck me!"

Lee obliged by thrusting inside her welcoming body. Tracy moaned, sighed and squealed in reply . . .

After Lee had ejaculated inside her, he pulled away and started to get dressed. Tracy raised herself to her knees and started to undress even more. "And where do you think you're going?"

She unzipped Lee again and pulled his Hamnett jeans and boxer shorts down. Her hands grasped his buttocks and her tongue lashed his penis. Lee smiled as he felt himself go hard again . . .

Kevin couldn't stop thinking about what Lee was doing to Sharon. She couldn't take this along with the violence. But how would she find out? He didn't have the heart to tell her, but she did have a right to know. Lee hadn't even phoned her to tell her about the aggro in Manchester.

Kevin backtracked to a call box around the corner from the pub. He checked up the street to see if there was any sign of Lee, but there wasn't anyone in sight.

"Hello?"

"Sharon? It's me Kev."

"Hiya! What time is it?"

"About midnight. I didn't know if you were out with your mates or not."

"Nah, Lee is supposed to be staying here tonight. Is he with you?"

"Er, no, sorry Sharon. He and some of the lads went to some party to celebrate the victory. I couldn't be bothered."

"Is he really drunk?"

"Well, yeah."

"Oh," she sighed, resigned to the fact.

"Sorry."

"It's okay. Anyway, what can I do for you since you phoned me?"

"Oh, nothing really, just checking you're okay."

"At this time? C'mon Kevin, I know you better than that. Do you fancy comin' over for a coffee?"

"Well, yeah, if you don't mind."

"I was waiting up for Lee anyway."

"Okay then, I'll be 'round shortly."

"See ya soon."

Kevin left the phone box, still in two minds whether or not to tell Sharon about Lee's antics with Tracy.

CHAPTER TEN

Kevin pushed the buzzer to Sharon's flat as he looked around to make sure Lee wasn't about.

"Hello?"

"It's me."

"C'mon up."

The door buzzer sounded and Kevin pushed though the front door and headed up the stairs two by two to Sharon's first floor flat. She was waiting for him on the landing.

"Hi, Kev."

"Yo, Sharon." Kevin smiled and followed her into her flat. He looked at her and thought how good she looked in the thigh length silk dressing gown with her hair all dishevelled.

"Coffee?" she asked.

"Yeah, please."

"You just go and make yourself comfortable and I'll bring it in."

Kevin went into the sitting room and sat on the settee. He lay his head back to gather his thoughts about the events of that day.

"C'mon sleepyhead!"

"Huh?" Kevin said, waking with a start. "Oh sorry, must have dozed off for a minute."

"It's okay. I made some toast in case you were hungry."

"Thanks, Sharon."

"So, how are you?"

"Not too bad, especially now I've got a coffee."

He smiled at Sharon who giggled and kissed him on the cheek. He turned to her and kissed her back, but pulled away quickly.

"Kev, did something happen today? You've gotta tell me." She grasped his arm urging him to tell her. Y'know Lee won't tell me if I ask him!"

"It wasn't that bad, honest."

"Tell me."

He put his arm around her shoulder and pulled her to him. Sharon responded by resting her head on his chest and placed her arm around his waist. Kevin told her everything - except the bit about Lee and Tracy.

"Every time he goes to the football now he gets into trouble!" she moaned.

"Tell me about it! I could live with the odd ruck now and again, but I can't keep up with 'im anymore."

"I'm just worried that one day he won't stop and someone will get hurt badly, y'know." Sharon sniffled a bit.

"Yeah, I know," Kevin said, holding her more tightly to comfort her. "It's telling 'im, that's the worst thing. He just refuses to listen."

"It's tearing me apart, I'm on the verge of givin' up. I don't think I love 'im anymore cos it hurts, really hurts!"

Kevin noticed the tears well up in her eyes.

"Thank God I've got you, Kevin." She kissed him on his jaw. "Someone I can really talk to. When I talk to my mates about Lee they just call me an idiot and tell me to leave 'im cos he's an animal. I'm beginning to think they're right." She looked up at him. "What are we going to do, Kev?"

"I wish I knew!"

He looked down into her eyes and realised how blue they were. He rubbed her shoulder comfortingly and Sharon leaned back onto his shoulder. Kevin still looked down at her. Sharon's gown had come apart slightly and he could see the deep cleavage that led to her shapely breasts. She moved, pulling her legs up onto the settee, and the movement caused the gown to fall even further apart, allowing Kevin to see her breasts.

Sharon looked up at Kevin again. Her right hand moved across her body and pulled the gown fully apart, exposing her breasts and shoulders. Kevin bent down and they kissed. His hand started to caress her breasts and he could feel her nipples go hard. Sharon unbuttoned his shirt and ran her hand across his well-toned body. She pulled away and stood up. She took his hands in hers and pulled him to his feet. He went to kiss her but she backed away, pulling him with her, until they'd reached the bedroom.

They stopped beside her bed. Sharon slipped off her gown and it landed at her feet. She took Kevin's shirt off and tossed it on the floor. He then pulled her to him and held her naked body in his arms as he kissed and nibbled her neck.

Sharon stepped back slightly and her fingers unbuttoned his jeans. She stood back from Kevin and he gazed at her. She pulled his jeans and shorts down, and Kevin slipped his trainers off and stepped out of his jeans. They looked each other up and down. Sharon thought how much more well built Kevin was compared to Lee. She could see the shape of all his muscles and the tan he still had after his Greek holiday with Lee.

Kevin noticed that Sharon must have been topless on her holiday. He raised his hands to her shoulders and slowly ran them down her body, feeling her skin tingle with goose bumps. He slowly pushed her to the bed and then knelt to where her feet were. He kissed every toe and then worked his way up her long legs. At the same time his hands ran over her body and her hands held his head. He kissed and licked his way up to her neck and then he kissed her lips.

Sharon responded to his excited body by rolling him over so he was on his back. She kissed her way down his body until she had his throbbing manhood in her mouth. After a while, she moved back up his body and straddled him, letting his manhood enter her. Her back stiffened in pleasure.

Kevin moaned, caressing her breasts as she moved up and down on him. He eventually rolled them both over and thrust into her. They pleased each other until neither of them could contain themselves, and they climaxed almost together. Their bodies glistened with sweat as Kevin pulled Sharon into his arms . . .

Sharon stirred slightly and Kevin woke up. The sound of the buzzer echoed around the silent flat until Sharon woke up too.

"Hmmm, what's that noise?" she asked sleepily.

"Oh, shit! It's your buzzer!"

"Oh God! Lee!"

Kevin leapt from the bed and hurriedly dressed, his shirt half buttoned up and the shirt tails hanging out. The buzzer rang again, but this time a few more times in urgent succession.

"I better answer it or else he'll go mad," Sharon said.

She headed for the intercom and Kevin looked frantically for another exit.

"He's on his way up!"

"Open the kitchen window," he said as he fumbled with his shoes.

"Why?"

"I'm going to go down the drainpipe."

"You could kill yourself!"

They heard a clatter and a drunken fit of laughter as Lee must have slipped on the stairs.

"It's better than being killed by him."

Sharon stood by the open window as Kevin swung out to the sound of Lee singing Chelsea victory songs.

"Be careful, Kevin." She grabbed hold of his arm as he faltered, and kissed him.

Kevin kissed her again and then slid out of her hands. She closed the window and peered into the darkness after Kevin. She dashed through to the front door just in time to let Lee in.

"Awright, Shaz!" He staggered and grabbed Sharon in a rough embrace. The smell of alcohol from Lee made Sharon turn her nose up.

He let go and headed into the bedroom. Sharon prayed that Kevin hadn't left anything and followed Lee to check. Lee just fell flat on his face on the bed and began snoring, so he wouldn't have noticed anything anyway. Sharon sighed with relief, and her thoughts turned to Kevin . . .

CHAPTER ELEVEN

Lee, as usual, arrived at the pub last. The lads greeted him as he made his way to the bar, and his grinning face advertised the fact that he had a few tricks up his sleeve. He found a drink already waiting for him and he winked at the shapely brunette barmaid to thank her.

"Can't get enough of these barmaids, eh?" Kevin said as he made his way over to Lee.

"Yo, Kev mate! How ya doin'? Looking forward to Germany then?"

"Too right, yeah! What's in the bag?"

"Just a present I've got for the lads." Lee said.

"Like what?"

"You're about to find out," Lee said with a mischievous look in his eye. "Right lads, gather 'round as I've got something for you."

An excited buzz filled the bar as Lee dipped his hand into the plain white plastic bag. The lads were swarming around him.

"What do you reckon to this then?" Lee held up a white t-shirt with a picture of two Cambodian soldiers carrying severed heads in each hand. CHELSEA CASUALS was emblazoned across the picture.

"Fuckin' excellent, Lee!" Terry said, grabbing it from him.

"Where the fuck did you get 'em?" John asked as he took his t-shirt from Lee.

The compliments continued to flow as Kevin looked on.

"Glad you like 'em, there's one for each of you. Including you, Joe."

"Thanks, Lee. You didn't have to. I mean, I ain't been with you lads for long."

"That don't matter, you're with us now and you'll be with us for the Germany game. You are one of the lads now cos I say so. 'Ere, Kev, what do you think?"

"What can I say, Lee." He was too stunned to say anything else.

"They're bloody wicked!" butted in Mike.

"Cheers, Mike."

"Yeah, wicked," Kev said with as much enthusiasm as he could muster. "When are we gonna wear 'em?"

"Well, Kev mate, we'll be donning these just before we arrive in Germany so they know the masters have arrived. It'll let the wimps from the other so called firms know that we've arrived."

A burst of laughter interrupted Lee and he looked over at the culprits. The sight made him laugh too and he nudged Kevin. The rest of the lads had their new t-shirts on over their already clothed bodies.

A white flash blinded Kevin as the shapely barmaid leaned over the bar to take photos. "Smile," she said, and the lads grinned at the vast cleavage resting of the bar.

Kevin sat quietly, leaving the rest of them to enjoy themselves.

Lee came over and joined him. "This is gonna be some fucking trip. No cunt is gonna mess with us! If they do they ain't gonna forget it in a hurry."

Lee brandished a brand new Stanley knife with CHELSEA engraved on the handle.

"Yeah, we're really gonna fuck 'em up!"

79

"Glad I can count on you. Kev, you should really think about getting one of these blades."

"Nah, fists and boots are enough for me. So what's the plan when we got there?" Kevin asked, gladly changing the subject.

"The usual. Let them know who's boss, beat a few heads into the ground, chase the local pigs around the streets, take a few souvenirs and get absolutely pissed!"

"Sounds good. I could do with knockin' a few empty heads together."

"Yeah, you and me, Kev. Partners in crime! We'll show 'em, eh?"

"Wanna drink Lee? Kevin?" Joe had wandered over to the table.

"Yeah, cheers Joe. Beers all 'round."

"What's going down then?"

"You just do as we do and you'll be fine. Just stick with me and Kev."

"Will do - can't wait!" Joe sounded cheerful, but he was secretly horrified by what was being planned. Terry had been telling him what usually happened on their trips abroad and it certainly wasn't in his job description.

Joe returned to the table just as Lee stood up and made for the pay phone.

"Cheer up, Kev!" he said, placing a pint down in front of him.

"Just psyching myself up for the ruck of the year, Joe, y'know."

"Yeah, sounds like fun. I'm really looking forward to my first trip away."

"Make the most of it, Joe, you'll never forget it."

"It'll be well catalogued, I can tell you."

"Watch what you do with that catalogued stuff," warned Kevin, "Cos if the coppers come sniffing around you could get lifted."

"No danger of that Kev, believe me!" said Joe.

"Kev! Kev! Someone get Kev! "

Kev looked up on hearing Lee's voice. "What is it, Lee?"

"'Ere, it's Shaz! Come and say cheerio! Cos I already have, know what I mean. Don't be too long, Kev! See ya babe!"

Kevin took the telephone handset and waited until Lee had joined the jubilant mob again.

"Sharon, how ya doin'?"

"Fine. Glad to hear your voice."

"You don't sound okay."

"I'm gonna finish with 'im when 'e comes back," she confided.

"Only if you're sure."

"Oh I don't know!" Sharon said with a sigh. "I saw those t-shirts - they're 'orrible!"

"Yeah, not very tasteful," Kevin said, looking over at the boys still wearing them. "I don't know if I can go through with this trip."

"Lee will kill you if you don't!"

"I know, but what else can I do? Fuck all!"

"Kevin?"

"Yeah?"

"Was the name of that copper that lifted you Welsh?"

"Yeah, how?"

"Don't get angry, but I bumped into him. Well, he bumped into me."

"What was he wantin'?" Kevin tried not to show his anger.

"He was asking about you and Lee and the rest of them. I said I didn't know anything."

"Good girl."

"He also gave me a message for you."

"Me?! What is it?"

"He said if you felt like a chat you should see a bloke called Joe Francis."

"Joe? Why Joe? He's only just joined us."

"Hasn't Welsh been watching you lot for a while?"

"That's what he says . . . " It suddenly dawned on Kevin what was going on, and the colour drained from his face. "Oh fuck! He's a bloody copper!"

"Be careful, Kevin. This Welsh must be wanting you pretty badly."

"Wanting to talk to me more likely. He's wanting to nail Lee. Listen, Sharon, I've gotta go. Lee's gettin' twitchy."

"Look after yourself and remember you don't have to do what Lee tells ya," Sharon said. "He's 'ad it comin' to 'im for a while."

"Not that way! I've gotta go, see ya Sharon."

"Yeah, see ya. Don't forget what I said." She blew a few kisses down the phone and hung up.

CHAPTER TWELVE

The plane began it's descent into Munich airport. It was late afternoon and the flight had been fairly quiet.

"Oi, Kev!" Lee said as he nudged him awake.

"Huh, yeah?"

"Awright?"

"Yeah, not bad."

"This is it! No going back now. The big one. We're gonna run the show out of here, not any of the idiots from the Red Army or Service Crew or any of the other mugs. A good show this time and the Chelsea will lead the national firm in the World Cup with me calling the shots."

So that's what this has been all about, Kevin thought. *Lee's gone power mad. Adolf Hitler wouldn't even get a look in with him around.*

On the bus from the airport to town, Lee was up at the front, scanning the streets for any signs of firms. Joe, meanwhile, had sat next to Kevin. "Alright? Good this innit. I'm really looking forward to tonight."

"Piss off!" Kevin hissed. "Or someone might just decide to grass you up!"

"And someone might just decide to put a word in a certain person's ear about your relationship with Sharon, know what I mean?"

Kevin's face dropped. *How on earth did he know! Shit, they must have been following me, and not Lee!*

Joe continued. "We've got enough on you to bang you up with Jones as an accessory, and we would make sure that you wouldn't last five minutes in the nick."

"We? What do you mean we? You've only just started coming with us. You don't know nothin'!"

"I may not have seen too much first hand, but Woolwich has seen the lot."

Fuckin' hell! Kevin's heart started to pound. Woolwich was a nickname for Ian, a quiet lad from Woolwich who had been with the firm for years. He kept himself to himself, but he'd always been around and seen everything. Kevin's thoughts were broken as Joe butted in.

"Think about it, Kevin. Talk to me and help me out and I'll help you out. See ya later."

The bus had come to a stop and Joe was now chatting to Lee up at the exit door.

What a scumbag, thought Kevin. His mind was in turmoil when he heard his name being called and he looked up.

Lee was grinning at him. "C'mon, Kev. Let's dump our stuff and go for a stroll to see what's what. Joe's comin' too."

"On my way," Kevin replied, getting to his feet.

The three of them left the bus and Lee pulled out a piece of paper. "Shaz found us a place to stay. I've given the address to the rest of the lads in case they get stuck for some place to kip."

"That Shaz of yours is some chick," said Joe, looking at Kevin as he spoke.

"She sure is, Joe, she sure is!"

"I haven't had the pleasure of meeting her yet."

"Well, when we get back I'll get her to come to one of the games."

"Will she not mind going to a game with all the lads?" Joe asked.

"Nah, she don't mind - she's used to the lads and the games we play! Ain't that right, Kev?"

"Yeah," Kev said, wishing they would talk about something else.

"My Shaz is one in a million, she'll do anything for me."

"What about that barmaid, what's her name?"

"Listen, Joe, what Shaz don't know won't hurt her, okay?" Lee glared at him to make sure he got the message.

"But what if she found out and decided to play the game your way?"

Lee stopped walking and stood in front of Joe. "What are you getting at, Joe?"

Kevin stared at them both, feeling a bit uneasy with the situation.

"Nothin', Lee, honest. I was just asking. I mean, y'know what some sorts are like."

"Well, Shaz ain't like that. She's crazy about me. Besides if any bastard lays one finger on her I'd kill 'im."

"Okay, okay! I'll drop the subject!" Joe said, raising his eyebrows in Kevin's direction.

"You just do that!" Lee replied sharply.

Kevin breathed a sigh of relief as they moved on towards their hotel. Joe turned towards him and smiled. Kevin glared back and swore under his breath.

"See that Joe has latched onto Lee in a big way."

"Yeah, it'd be funny if he puts Kev's nose out of joint!"

Terry and John laughed as they headed into town to check out the pubs.

"'Ere, Tel, what do you make of Kev these days?"

"Dunno, sometimes 'e's alright and other times 'e's a right bore. Don't get me wrong. I like the geezer, but he pisses me off sometimes."

"I wonder what's got into 'im cos 'e's pissing Lee off too. Mind you, they've been mates for years so Lee'll sort 'im out."

"Hope so, for all our sakes! What about Joe?"

"What about 'im?"

"Precisely! Comes from fuckin' nowhere an' all of a sudden 'e's flavour of the month!"

"Yeah, but 'e seems pretty game," admitted Terry.

"True. 'Ere let's try this place - looks okay."

They headed into a traditional looking beer cellar.

"We'll soon see what Joe's made of on this trip," said John as they approached the bar.

"Kev too," added Terry as he attracted the barman's attention. "Two steiners, mate," he said, holding up two fingers and pointing to the beer pump.

CHAPTER THIRTEEN

Lee put on his Ralph Lauren jacket and checked his wallet. He dipped into the inside pocket again and pulled out his Stanley knife.

"You won't be needing that tonight, Lee," Kevin said. "We're only going for a few beers and a laugh."

"You never know who we'll meet out there, and I want to be prepared."

Kevin shook his head and decided not to push the issue. Joe looked on with interest.

"Okay, who wants to look after the keys?" Lee asked, putting his arm around Joe's shoulders. "Cos I don't know if I'll be back or not."

"How not?"

"Joe, we're over here to teach these German bastards a lesson," Lee explained. "So tonight I might be showing some of the local bitches what us Cockney lads are really made of, get my meaning?"

"Oh, right."

"Yeah right. Kev, you ready?"

"Yeah, let's go. Give me the keys. I'm saving my energy for tomorrow."

"Here you go," Lee said. "I'm sure you're going soft though, mate."

"How?"

"Not bedding a German tart. I don't think you've shagged another bird since you split with Karen and that was a few months back."

"Yeah, well, I'll see," Kev said, his eyes glaring at the grin on Joe's face.

After leaving the hotel and heading for the red light district, Lee, Kevin and Joe ended up in a huge beer cellar. The waitresses were dressed up in three quarter length gingham dresses and frilly aprons, and they carried three steiners of beer in each hand and slung them down on the tables. The ompah band in the corner, dressed in old country costume, blasted out old folk tunes while the customers sat on long benches and swayed to the rhythm of the music. The England fans, already full of beer, took turns to dance on the tables.

"This place is wild!" Joe had to shout to be heard.

"Too right! Good cheap beer and good company!" Lee turned and pinched the backside of a waitress as she squeezed passed. She twisted her head around and Lee winked and raised his Steiner to her, but she carried on past.

Lee and Kevin clashed their steiners together, beer sloshing over the table. The ompah band went quiet, but the punters continued to dance on the tables and fool around. As the band tuned up for their next offering, it soon became clear to the English lads what they were playing. The dancing and swaying stopped and the joking and laughing came to an abrupt halt. Steiners crashed onto the tables as *Deutschland Uber Alles* pounded out from the small stage.

"Fuckin' bastards!" Lee hurled his Steiner across the cellar as the English contingent began booing the band. "C'mon Kev, Joe, let's finish this place!"

He grabbed another Steiner and threw it towards the band. A number of other lads followed suit as they jumped to their feet and started to attack the locals. Kevin grabbed the table and turned it over, sending beer and glass flying everywhere.

"Steady on, Kevin!"

"Listen, Joe, I ain't gonna let a bunch of German bastards get the better of me! I think you ought to do the same if you want to keep in with Lee."

"Yeah, right." Joe turned and started to hurl anything that was within reach, but he made sure he missed all of his targets.

Kevin spotted a young lad trying to crawl to the nearest exit. He ran over, picked up an ashtray and crashed it across the lad's head. Then he aimed his Puma State at his body. He booted him several times, but stopped when he heard whistling and shouting. The police had arrived and the beer cellar was no longer the place to be. Not if you were English anyway.

Kevin looked around, trying to find Lee, but he only saw Joe up near the stage doing more watching than taking part. "Where's Lee?" he asked after making his way over.

"Dunno, that's who I'm looking for."

"We're gonna have to get outta here before the coppers catch up with us."

"It's a bit late for that, Kevin."

"Very funny! Now look for Lee and quick!"

"Okay, okay!"

They looked through the melee of low flying steiners and arms and legs taking aim. Lee was thrashing into a semi-conscious German. The lad was held against the wall with Lee's left hand while his right hand pummelled the limp body and sagging head. A hand grabbed Lee's shoulder and he twisted around with anger blazing in his eyes.

"Fuck's sake, Joe!" Lee shouted.

"We gotta move, the coppers are here!"

Lee let go of his prey and the lad crumpled to the ground.

Joe just looked from the lad to Lee. "Christ, what a mess!"

"Yeah, he deserved it. Where's Kev?"

"Over there."

They made their way to Kevin who was trying to smash through a fire exit with a chair. By now the police were swarming all over the place, grabbing everyone in sight. Kevin caught a glimpse of a truncheon, and so twisted around and walloped the copper with the chair.

"Nice one, Kev," Lee said. "Is that door open?"

"Dunno, I think it's stuck."

The pair of them shouldered the door and eventually it gave way. They stumbled into an alley and Joe followed them as they ran down towards a main road. With the beer cellar a good few streets away now, they paused in a shop doorway to catch their breath.

"I seen what you did to that copper, Kev," Lee said, breathing heavily still.

"If I hadn't got him he would've got me, and I don't wanna be nicked!"

"Hey, I ain't criticising. Just as I think you're losin' it, you produce the goods." Lee laughed and crouched down.

"What's so funny?" Joe asked.

"That was some ruck, and we got away with it again."

"Yeah, the Old Bill didn't stand a chance of getting us," Kevin said. And then for the benefit of Joe, he added, "They never do."

"So Joe, if you don't wanna get nicked stick with us." Lee grinned and slapped Joe on the back.

"We better get going," Kevin said, leaving the safety of the doorway to look up and down the street. "This area will be swamped with coppers soon."

They straightened up and dusted themselves down. Lee looked up and down the street too, but there wasn't any sign of the police - just the distant wail of sirens.

"Let's try the other end of town and see what's going on down there," Lee said as they headed off in the opposite direction to the sirens.

The bouncers looked them up and down, and then opened the door to a dark and smoky club. They paid the dolled-up tart standing at the till, and walked through to the bar. They could see a few English lads dancing and drinking, but it all seemed quiet and oblivious to the trouble kicking off in other clubs around the town.

Kevin headed towards the bar and ordered up a round.

A young girl sidled up to him. "Do you have a light?"

"Yeah, sure," he said, lighting her cigarette.

"You English?"

"Yeah."

"I like English men," she said, her eyes giving Kevin the biggest come on he'd ever been party to. "You have somewhere to sleep tonight?"

"Oi, Kev, you chatting up the local birds already?" Lee asked after seeing why it was taking so long to get a beer. "You ain't wastin' any time!"

"I don't think she's a local bird. I think she's the kind you have to pay for."

"Yeah? Awright darlin'?"

"You English too?"

"The best Englishman you'll ever meet." Lee put his arm around her waist and pulled her towards him.

"You buy me a drink?"

"Anythin' you want, you get. Kev, get a drink for the little lady." Lee looked the prostitute up and down and smiled.

"You like?"

"I sure do," Lee said, taking her hand. "Let's go sit down."

"Well, that leaves you and me, Kev," Joe said, as he watch Lee and the girl walk over to a small booth in a corner of the club.

"Unfortunately. We may as well get a seat too. I think that's a couple of Chelsea lads over there - it'll give me someone to talk to."

"There's no need to be like that Kevin, I'm only doing a job."

"I don't fuckin' care what you're doing," Kevin snapped. "Now let's go."

A few drinks later, Lee made his way over to where Kevin and Joe were sitting. "Won't be coming back with you tonight, boys," he said with a grin.

"No need to ask where you're going."

"Aw, Kev, this tart is gorgeous! Big tits, long legs and a tongue that would put a snake to shame."

"Enjoy." *Bastard, he can't wait to dive into someone else's bed. He doesn't give a damn about Sharon.*

"Will do," Lee said with a knowing wink. "Who's this you're with?"

"Chelsea."

"Yeah? Haven't seen 'em around."

"They're normal fans, y'know, colours an' that."

"Right, see you two tomorrow."

Kevin shook his head as Lee sauntered back to the tart.

"What's wrong, Kevin?" Joe asked.

"Nothin'."

"Doesn't look like nothin'."

"Well it is, Joe. Lee's away with that tart so we'll see him tomorrow."

"What about Sharon?"

"What about her?" Kevin was getting fed up with Joe's constant stream of questions.

"What would she say about all this?"

"Nothin', cos she ain't gonna find out, is she."

"You really fancy her, eh?"

"Fancy her? No, I care for her and she deserves better than the likes of Lee."

"You mean you," Joe said, picking up his beer.

"At least I'm not a maniac."

"You ready to talk then?"

"Fuck off!" Kevin turned away and joined in the conversation with the other Chelsea fans.

Lee stood at the table and nodded his head towards the door. The prostitute finished her drink and stood up. She pulled her skirt down so it covered the top of her stockings and straightened her top so her cleavage could be seen more clearly. Lee pulled her towards him and squeezed her buttocks and thrust his crotch to hers. She smiled and led him out of the club.

They ended up at a seedy bedsit. The door struggled to fit into the frame and the damp was chasing the wallpaper down the wall.

"You live here?" Lee asked, thinking he wouldn't keep a dog in a place like this.

"Sometimes. Sometimes I go home to my parents, but they are ashamed of me so I don't stay for long. Sometimes I stay with friends who do the same job as me."

"What's your name?"

"Anna. What is your name?"

"Lee." He stood in front of her and took his jacket off. They kissed as he ran his hands down over her breasts. He roughly groped at them and almost tore her blouse open.

Anna pulled away and took the blouse off.

Lee looked down. "And the rest."

She wriggled out of her tight mini skirt and kicked off her stilettos. She stood in front of Lee dressed in a half cup bra, crotchless panties, stockings and suspenders.

Lee smiled as he unbuttoned his Armani jeans. He pulled out his erect manhood and Anna knelt down and started to lick and suck. Lee grabbed her hair as she bobbed up and down.

As she worked away, Lee looked around the room and saw an array of sexual extras. He pulled her head away from his throbbing dick.

Anna smiled up at him. "You like?"

"Yeah, but how about something kinky?"

"It costs extra."

"Fair enough," Lee said, his hand running through her hair. "Do you do watersports?"

Anna was slightly surprised at the strange request. "Are you sure? You don't strike me as the submissive type."

"You can't judge a book by the cover. I've always been dominant and since this won't be found out, I fancy a change. Now, how much?"

"The whole night will be 150 marks."

"Fair enough, now do it."

Anna pushed Lee onto his back and squatted over his face. She ground her pussy over his face. "Lick me!"

She gasped as Lee's tongue brushed against her clitoris. After a few minutes and as the excitement heightened, Anna felt her orgasm approaching.

"I'm coming!" she yelled, grinding her crotch harder into Lee's face. "Open your mouth - I'm going to piss."

As the orgasm swept over her, Anna felt the tightening of her bowels, and gradually began to release the warm liquid, directing it into Lee's mouth.

This is gonna be some night and this bitch ain't never gonna get the likes of me again!

CHAPTER FOURTEEN

As he walked in with Joe, Kevin was surprised to see Lee already in the pub where Chelsea had arranged to meet that day.

"Awright Kev?" Lee called out, his face beaming with the pleasures of the night before.

"Get the beers in Joe," said Kevin as he walked over to where Lee was sitting. "How did you get on last night then?"

"Magic, she was well kinky. She liked it rough."

"Yeah? She is okay though - you didn't beat her too badly?" Kevin had visions of her lying dead in a back alley somewhere.

"She's awright," said Lee, which was more than could be said for him. The weals on his back still burned from the whipping he had received.

Kevin's concern for the condition of the girl was interrupted when a few more Chelsea walked into the pub and began exchanging notes about their escapades the previous night.

Over at the bar, Kevin noticed Ian and Joe in deep conversation. No *prizes for guessing what they're talking about!* he thought to himself. Uncertainty at what to do swept over him once again. Half of him wanted to grass them to Lee and the rest of the firm, and then bluff it out about his relationship with Sharon. But deep down, something was telling him that the violence had gotten way too serious, and despite it being totally against the grain, he wanted to help the Old Bill.

Kevin, still deep in thought, subconsciously felt the atmosphere change in the pub. When he looked up, he noticed that around 30 lads belonging to Arsenal's firm had walked into the pub. Kevin recognised one of the lads from the North Bank when Chelsea were in there earlier in the season.

"Awright Skeets," Lee called out to a large Jamaican youth, one of the main faces at Highbury.

Skeets grinned over. "Yo bro. We wondered where you lot had got to."

The atmosphere relaxed as the youths began to mingle. How two groups of hooligans, normally at each others throats, could call a truce at an England match never failed to amaze Kevin. Although such truces were generally observed, they didn't occur in every situation. West Ham's firm didn't like to mingle with the other London mobs, and there was often a bit of tension between Northern and Southern firms too, especially Chelsea and Leeds. Already some of the Arsenal boys were telling of how Portsmouth's crew had been fighting with rival Southampton lads in the town centre the previous night.

All afternoon, the England firm's numbers increased as other hooligans turned up - most notably a group of around 40 Millwall who arrived to some friendly slagging. As usual Chelsea, Millwall and Arsenal made up the bulk of England's mob. Veterans of many a riot in Europe, the three gangs had often fought side by side, bound by national pride, on a number of occasions now.

As 6pm approached, drinks were finished and the alcohol-fuelled bodies walked out into the evening air, full of anticipation for the night ahead.

An unmarked police van was parked across the road from the pub. Inside were German police officers and two members of the Football Intelligence Unit.

"The usual alliance has been struck up I see," said DS Moss to his colleague DC Johnston.

"Yeah Sarge, and there's the covert officer with Jones. They're the main troublemakers in this group. If you keep this lot under observation we should be okay." He turned to the German officers. "Any other trouble that breaks out will be minor and probably only a result of excess alcohol and should be easy to control."

The Germans nodded in acknowledgement. Although they were beginning to suffer from football hooliganism in their own domestic league programme, it was nowhere near as premeditated as this. However, they had prepared well and had mounted one of the largest police operations in the city's history to prevent the trouble. The van started up and slowly tailed the tramcar that the hooligans had piled into en route to the stadium.

When the England fans got off the tram, they were immediately surrounded and outnumbered by German riot police who had been tipped off by the unmarked van that trouble was on its way.

"Fuckin' 'ell!" Lee complained. "There's not much chance of an off beforehand."

"Yeah it looks as if the Old Bill have rumbled us," said Kevin as he looked over at Joe, who smiled back in return.

"Still, there will be enough opportunities to have a go tonight, after the match," said Lee perking up. "They've never stopped us before, 'ave they? We've always managed to kick off."

Who's worrying, thought Kevin as nagging doubts about remaining involved in the football scene returned.

A German mounted policeman advised the England fans that they would be escorted straight to the ground and that any fans without tickets would be able to pay cash at the gates.

So much for the FA's threat that ticketless fans would be refused admission, Joe thought as the line of fans was marched into the pen reserved for England supporters.

The atmosphere inside the ground was electric as the teams ran onto the pitch. All the lads had positioned themselves at the top of the terracing next to the fence that separated them from the Germans. Although the ground was all seated, almost everyone in the England section was standing.

RULE BRITANNIA!

BRITANNIA RULE THE WAVES!

BRITONS NEVER NEVER NEVER SHALL BE SLAVES!

TWO WORLD WARS AND ONE WORLD CUP!

ENGLAND! ENGLAND!

The songs echoed around the ground as the game kicked off at a furious pace. England were on top for most of the first half, but disaster struck when Germany caught England on the break and scored the opening goal just before half time.

"Bastards!" shouted Lee as the Germans celebrated wildly on the other side of the fence.

Kevin looked around the mob. Nobody was watching the game as the half time whistle went. Everyone was glaring at the Germans through the fence.

Suddenly a flare was fired by the Germans deep into the England supporters. Luckily it didn't hit anyone, but it was all that was needed to kick things off and the England supporters reacted violently. Seats were being kicked out and thrown over into the German end, and the various firms tried to scale the fences.

The police moved in, hitting out with their riot sticks, and Kevin noticed Lee being dragged away by two officers. Without thinking he rushed to his friend's aid, hitting one of the policemen with a plastic seat. "Do the Old Bill!" he screamed as some normal England supporters looked on unsure.

With their adrenaline flowing, Kevin's words of encouragement saw ordinary fans join seasoned hooligans in attacking the police and chasing them down towards the pitch.

"Cheers lads," muttered a slightly dazed Lee who had managed to break free as the police retreated. He looked at Kevin and smiled weakly. "That's one I owe you, Kev."

"Anything for a mate," Kev said. *Once again I've shown that my loyalties are with Lee. Maybe I should have a word with that Joe when I get the chance, and tell him it's no deal. I'll speak to him when he's on his own. At least that way it gives him and Woolwich a chance to get clear before I tell Lee.*

Satisfied that his mind was made up at last, he turned his attention to the teams coming onto the pitch for the second half.

CHAPTER FIFTEEN

The police eventually opened the gates to let the England fans leave the otherwise deserted stadium a full 45 minutes after the final whistle. Kevin walked alongside Lee at the front of the England fans as the police led them into a caged pen to wait for coaches to take them back into the town centre.

Lee walked over to the other side of the pen and tested the gate. To his amazement he found that it wasn't locked, and there weren't any police at that side of the pen either.

"Oi Skeets, this is unlocked," he whispered to the Arsenal lad. "Get everyone up this end."

"Cool!" the black youth replied, and he passed the message around.

Everyone slowly began to bunch up around the gate without the police noticing.

"Come on England!" yelled a Millwall lad as he kicked the gate open.

Everyone surged through and before the police had a chance to react, the charging mob had disappeared into the pitch darkness of a park which surrounded the concourse. The German police had allowed them to disappear into the night.

"That's blown it Sarge," said DC Johnston still inside the unmarked van. "It's going to be a busy night now."

DS Moss nodded in agreement. "How could the Germans slip up like that?"

"Bleedin' amateurs!" Johnston muttered as the van lurched off in an attempt to find the gang.

"There's a main road - let's get onto that!" Lee shouted Lee.

"Spread out when we get onto the road!" added Skeets. "And keep the noise down!"

The gang slowed down as they reached the road.

Lee looked behind him to get an idea of numbers. "There must be about a hundred of us here, Kev. More than enough."

Kevin nodded with nervous excitement.

"Look, there's a target down there," said a youth wearing an Armani sweatshirt with a small Manchester United pin badge attached.

Lee and Skeets looked to where the lad was pointing. A pub that had German fans drinking outside.

"That'll do for starters," Lee said as the gang began to cross the road.

The German drinkers noticed the approaching mob and called into the pub for reinforcements. They were quickly joined by others armed with beer tumblers and bar stools.

"Come on ya German bastards! Let's go!" shouted Mad Mike as he ran straight into a group of Germans, fists flying.

All hell broke loose as the Germans counter-attacked with bottles and glasses. Lee and Kevin stood back to back, fighting the Germans tooth and nail. Kevin eventually turned to check on Lee and saw him in the doorway of the pub surrounded by Germans armed with stools. Adrenaline-fuelled rage engulfed him as he ran to help.

And then there was a flash of metal.

A German youth staggered backwards, falling over as he tried to hold his face together.

Both Kevin and the German youths backed away from Lee who lunged again with the blade. The Germans turned and started to flee, leaving the stab victim on the ground. Enraged that his prey were escaping, Lee fell onto the grounded German, slashing into the youth's body.

"No Lee! Stop!" Kevin yelled, pulling at his friend's sleeve. "You're gonna to kill 'im!"

Lee swung around with the knife, just missing Kevin's chest. "Fuck off Kev, or I'll do you as well!" Lee snarled, his face twisted with hatred as he turned back to the German youth.

Kevin stood back, appalled at what he was witnessing.

The sound of police sirens over the constant noise of breaking glass signalled that it was time to get away from the area.

"C'mon Kevin, let's get outta here!" Joe grabbed Kevin and started to pull him in the opposite direction to the sirens.

"What are you bothered about! They're your kind ain't they?!" Kevin shook off Joe's grasp.

"Keep your voice down! I don't want everyone to know Kevin!"

"Typical! Let's go!"

A few of the firm started to run, and Kevin and Joe went with them, leaving Lee behind. Deep down, Kevin hoped that the police would nick him.

* * *

Lee was down on one knee, with his left arm resting on his knee and his right arm going up and down like a piston. He could hear voices, possibly shouts, but they swam around his head without really registering. The faces around him blurred as his determination to teach the enemy a lesson in English dominance totally dominated his thoughts.

The knife continued to slide in and out with ease and he grinned. He felt something hit his face and stopped his attack so he could run his fingers across his cheek.

He looked down at his hand and saw the blood. "You German bastard! How dare you bleed on me!"

He was about to take aim again when he heard something other than the voices in his head - police sirens.

"Damn it!" Lee wiped the blade and his hand on the jeans of his motionless enemy and ran for it.

* * *

As the fleeing firm made some distance from the coppers they started to split up into small groups. Kevin glanced around and ducked in with Skeets as he saw Joe heading off with some Millwall boys. *Thank fuck for that!*

CHAPTER SIXTEEN

The next morning, Kevin awoke in the hotel room and looked around. Joe must have come in during the night as he was sleeping on the next bed, but there was no sign of Lee. *Hope the bastard got nicked*, he thought as he quietly got dressed, trying not to wake Joe.

"I'm finished with all this," he muttered to himself as he walked past the reception desk. The hotel had made all England fans pay their bill in advance so there was no problem in leaving.

As he walked through the hotel lobby, he noticed Lee curled up like a baby on one of the settees, fast asleep. He hadn't been arrested after all. *That settles it! I'm gonna try to get an earlier flight home. Fuck Lee. I ain't putting up with knife attacks.*

At the airport Kevin made his way toward the British Airways booking desk. "Hi, I'm booked on the 17:30 hours flight to London Heathrow tonight and was wondering if it was possible to change my ticket to get on an earlier flight." He handed over his ticket to the blonde stewardess.

"I'll have a look for you, sir," smiled the potential Miss World behind the desk.

As she bent over her VDU, Kevin had a first class view down her blouse. He straightened up and grinned, and then blushed as he realised that she wasn't wearing a bra.

The woman looked up, catching Kevin in the act and smiled at his embarrassment. "Yes, sir, that's no problem." *A nice looking lad,* she thought to herself as she punched the details into the VDU. *Probably one of these football hooligans though.* "I can get you on the 09:45 flight which gives you only 45 minutes to get your boarding card and clear customs. Will that be okay?"

"That's fine, thanks."

"Welcome to London Heathrow."

The air hostess' announcement woke Kevin from his fitful slumber. As he walked off the plane, it felt great to be back home again. The feeling of happiness doubled knowing that each step he took was a step away from the world of football violence.

After clearing customs successfully, he walked into WH Smith to catch up on the news.

YOUTH STABBED TO DEATH
AS ENGLAND FANS RIOT
ENGLAND FANS SHAME AS GERMAN FAN DIES
MURDERERS!

The front page headline of every tabloid newspaper screamed at Kevin. His hands were trembling as he picked up one of the 'papers and took it over to the cashier. Cold sweat ran down his back as he read the report which confirmed that it was the same incident that he was at.

Lee was a murderer. His best mate for years, a murderer, and he, Kevin, had watched it happen and then ran away doing nothing. "What the fuck am I gonna do!" he said out loud.

107

He walked stunned into the airport lobby. His eyes rested on some objects on the opposite wall. Payphones. Sharon.

"Hi, Sharon, it's Kevin."

"Hi, Kev! Where are you phoning from?"

"Heathrow."

"When did you get back? I didn't think you lot were due back until tonight."

"About 'alf an hour ago. Look, I need to see you, like now."

"Yeah, okay. Is Lee with you?"

"Nah, look Sharon I'll see you in about an hour."

"Kevin . . . "

It was too late. He had already hung up and was almost sprinting towards the tube.

The tube journey seemed to take an eternity as the events of the last couple of days unfolded in his mind. There's was no doubt that Lee shouldn't be allowed to get away with murder. He had to talk to DI Welsh, but he couldn't do that. His friendship with Lee surely still counted for something. He could speak to Lee and make him see sense. Make him see that they could still run riot without killing anyone.

But what if that didn't work. Lee would go daft at him! *Shit! Why me? I didn't deserve all this hassle? It wasn't worth it!*

Kevin rested his head in his hands and tried to collect his thoughts, but it didn't work. Visions of the German youth dead on the ground continued to play on his mind.

The constant noise of the buzzer started to hurt Sharon's ears as she made her way to the hall.

"Hello? Kevin?"

"Yeah."

She released the main door and Kevin virtually burst through it and bolted up the stairs. Sharon stared in amazement at the speed Kevin was travelling at. When he reached her at the landing, he dropped his holdall and took Sharon in his arms and held her tightly.

Sharon returned the affection, but could feel Kevin trembling. She pulled away and looked up into his face. There was despair written all over it and anguish filled his eyes. "Kevin, what's wrong?"

"Oh God, Sharon." He pulled her back into his arms and buried his face in her hair. For the first time in years he felt like crying.

"We better get in, Kev."

"Yeah, c'mon."

Sharon pulled Kevin inside and closed the door. Kevin's shoulders had an unusual slump about them as he slowly made his way to her living room.

When she got there Kevin was sitting with his head in his hands. "You look like you need a coffee."

"Got anything stronger?"

"Whisky?"

"Yeah, make it a large one."

Sharon went to her small drinks cabinet and poured an extra large whisky into a tumbler. She sat beside Kevin and put one arm around his waist and handed him his drink.

"Thanks, Sharon, I need this."

He gulped almost all of it in one go.

"Easy! Now tell me what's wrong."

Kevin reached into his holdall and pulled out the 'paper he had bought at the airport. "Check out the front page."

She took the 'paper and unfolded it. Her eyes looked over the headline, but it didn't register at first. She read it again and then went onto the article on the inside. The more she read the more it sunk in. She looked to Kevin. "Lee?"

"Yeah."

"Oh my God!"

The 'paper fell to the floor as her hands flew to her face. The colour drained from her as the image of Lee stabbing someone to death flooded her mind. "Are you sure?"

"I was there, I saw it happen, and I didn't do nothin' . . . Just ran when the coppers arrived."

"Oh Kevin! Did he get arrested?"

"Did he fuck! When I left the hotel this morning he was fast asleep in the lobby and I wasn't about to wake 'im."

The two of them sat in silence for what seemed like hours.

"Are you okay?" Sharon eventually asked.

"Yeah, a bit tired, but I'll survive."

"Go to bed then."

Kevin smiled and patted her thigh. "Sorry, don't have much energy at the moment."

Sharon giggled and held his hand. "Not for that silly, for a sleep!"

"Sounds like a good idea," he admitted.

"Just go through," she said, kissing him on the forehead. "I'll wake you in a few hours."

"Are you sure?"

110

"Yes! Now go on!" She pulled him off the settee and pushed him towards her bedroom.

Kevin started to undress and Sharon drew the curtains. She turned to see Kevin's back as he was pulling his jeans off. She saw all his muscles tense and relax as he finished undressing.

Kevin sat on the side of the bed and yawned. "Wanna join me?"

She walked over to the bed and sat beside him. "I didn't think you had the energy."

"I don't. Just fancy the company."

"Okay then."

He turned to face her and kissed her. She put her arms around his neck and kissed him back. Kevin pulled her close and he felt Sharon run her hands down his back. "Comin' to bed dressed like that?"

Sharon laughed as she stood up. Kevin slid under the duvet and watched Sharon undress and join him in bed. They held each other in silence and it wasn't long before both of them were asleep.

CHAPTER SEVENTEEN

"Anyone seen Kev?" Lee was frantically asking anyone and everyone the same question.

"Must've done a runner, Lee!" Terry sniggered.

Lee grabbed him. "Fuckin' watch it, Tel!"

"Okay, okay! Only kiddin'!"

"You better be!" He let go of Terry's jacket and Terry dusted the creases out. "Who saw him last?"

Mike tried to keep the situation calm. "Joe did."

"Where?"

"After that ruck we had at that first pub," Mike said.

"Where's Joe now?"

"He's over there, seein' if Skeets or any of the others have seen 'im."

"He can't be far."

"Could be with some slag!"

"Yeah, John could be right, Lee."

"It's a possibility but 'e would've turned up by now."

The firm looked around blankly, not knowing what to say. Lee went across to see if Joe was having any luck.

"If you ask me, Kev's done a runner," Terry said to John quietly.

"You don't know that for sure, Terry."

"Yeah, so where is he then John, eh? His bottle crashed at that ruck last night and he scampered."

"Not Kev, 'is loyalty lies with Lee. Always has done, always will do."

"Well, I don't think so. Kev's been losin' it for a while."

"I don't think so, Terry. Kev's still game."

"Awright, what about Arsenal, Man U, and the scuffles at the club? What about then?"

John looked to the ground knowing Terry was right, but he liked Kevin and didn't want to face what could be the truth.

"C'mon lads, this ain't gettin' us anywhere." Mike came to the rescue again as he spotted Lee and Joe coming back to join them. "Any luck, Joe?"

"Nah, me and Skeets seem to be the last ones to see 'im."

"When?"

"After the coppers arrived last night, me and Kevin made a break for it cos we didn't want to get nicked."

"Where did you go?"

"Just headed down the street and split up. He went off with Skeets and I ended up with some Millwall."

"Unlucky!" Mike joked, trying to ease the atmosphere.

"And?" Terry was waiting for the opportunity to slag Kevin off again.

"According to Skeets they got into a few scuffles later on, but the coppers were everywhere and next thing he knew, Kevin had disappeared."

"Disappeared?" Terry said, still clueless.

"Fuck!" Lee exclaimed. "He's been lifted! I heard a few lads had been lifted last night, and Kev must be one of 'em."

Lee's face reddened in anger, and Terry's face dropped at the thought of Kevin getting another hero's welcome when he got out. Lee hurled his glass through the nearest window and the bar went silent. The policemen outside ducked to avoid the splinters of glass.

113

"Don't move." DS Moss prayed the German police would keep their cool and just let the last few incidents pass over.

"What time is their flight, Sarge?"

"Some off them are on the 17:30, but unfortunately some of them will be heading to the train station to catch the overnight ferry. With any luck, this lot won't be up to anything much now. I think they got it out their system last night."

"Yeah, the Germans made a number of arrests."

"What are they doing about them?"

"Deportation," Johnston replied, knowing that Moss wanted to hear they were being prosecuted, not let off yet again.

"Did you manage to get a list of names?"

"Yeah, here you go."

The DS took the list and looked down it, shaking his head. "I see it's the same old crowd. Luckily they didn't lift any of our own. But it's a shame they didn't nail that murdering bastard!"

"Any idea who done it?" the DC asked.

The word is it could be one of the Chelsea lads. Possible the mob Francis is in with. But we won't know until he gets back."

"Shame."

"Yeah. Hold up, isn't that Jones leaving the pub?"

Johnston looked over at the group of England fans standing on the pavement. "I think so, Sarge, and he's looking pretty pissed off about something too."

"Hmm, I wouldn't mind knowing what about."

The two of them watched intently, trying to pick up some clue to Lee's anger.

Lee looked around for something or someone to release his frustration and anger on. He spotted the van and was sure he'd seen it before. "'Ere, does anyone recognise that van?"

Some of them did, but all from different places at different times.

"Bet it's the Old Bill!"

"Just what I was thinking, John." Lee walked into the middle of the street and stood facing the van. He picked up a stone and threw it. The others followed suit, but were pushed back by the German police who had been standing outside the pub all day.

"C'mon Lee. We better get goin' before we all get nicked." Mike pulled Lee back and tried to calm him down.

"Yeah, you're right. C'mon lads let's get outta this fuckin' city!"

The firm turned and swaggered away from the situation and towards home. As they did so, one more stone was thrown, bouncing off the van's roof.

"Pig bastards!"

CHAPTER EIGHTEEN

The early evening sunlight was peeping through a crack in the curtains when Sharon woke up. Kevin was in her arms and fast asleep. She eased her body from the bed and he stirred slightly, but didn't wake up.

Sharon slipped on her dressing gown and went through to the living room. She sat down and picked up the 'paper Kevin had bought. She still couldn't believe it, but deep down she knew it was true. Every time Lee got into trouble he was stepping up a gear, and stabbing someone was a logical next step.

She went through to the kitchen and put the kettle on. She sat at the breakfast bar, waiting for it to boil, trying to get things right in her mind. She glanced around her kitchen and her eyes rested on her cork pinboard. She frowned at a small insignificant piece of paper that seemed to stick out, then she slipped from the stool and went across to the pinboard. She removed the pin and read the scrawled writing: "DI Jim Welsh, Fulham CID."

"That's it! That's the answer!"

The kettle came to the boil, but stopped as Sharon pulled the plug.

"Could I speak to DI Welsh please?"

"Who's calling?"

"Just tell 'im it's about Lee Jones."

"Hold the line a minute."

Sharon waiting for less than 20 seconds before a male voice came on the line.

"DI Welsh."

116

"Hello, it's Sharon. Sharon Gillespie."

"Ah, Miss Gillespie! To what do I owe this pleasure?" His mouth went into a face splitting grin as he leaned back in his chair and swung his feet onto his desk.

"It's about Lee," Sharon said quietly.

"I thought as much."

"Y'know he went over to Germany for the football? Well . . . " She paused as a moment of guilt swept across her.

"Well, what?" he asked impatiently.

"Don't push me! This ain't easy!"

"Okay, okay, now calm down and tell me what you were going to say."

"Well, a German fan was stabbed to death last night and Lee did it."

"His feet flew to the floor as Welsh sat bolt up right. "What?"

"You 'eard."

"Jones stabbed that youth?! How do you know? Did he tell you?"

"No, I haven't seen 'im. I don't think he's due back until tonight. Kevin told me."

"Kevin Murray? Isn't he with Jones?"

"No, he came back this morning cos he wanted to get away from Lee."

Welsh couldn't believe his ears. "How does Kevin know?"

"He was there, he saw Lee do it."

"Where is Kevin now?"

"Here with me."

"Is he coming to see me then?" Welsh really did want everything on a plate.

117

"I dunno. He doesn't now that I've called you."

"Hmmm. Do you think he will come and see me?"

"I dunno! He's pretty messed up about all of it."

"Would you be able to make him come in?" Welsh knew that if anyone was going to talk Kevin around to shopping his best mate it had to be Sharon.

"Dunno, I could try."

"Good girl! What's brought on this change of heart then, Sharon?"

"None of your business!" she snapped. "All I know is Lee has turned into an animal and shouldn't be on the streets."

"Okay, okay! Just work on Kevin for me and let me know what he's decided."

"Okay, I'll see what I can do."

Welsh smugly hung up the phone and laughed to himself. He stood up, walked out of his office and into the CID room.

"What's the joke, Guv?" asked one of the officers.

"As soon as Francis sets foot in England get him to make a report straight away!"

"What's the hurry, Guv?"

"Jones killed that German lad."

"You're kidding!"

The CID officers went silent in disbelief.

"How did you find out?" asked a Detective Sergeant.

"Well, Sergeant, his girlfriend - well, ex-girlfriend now - has just phoned to tell me! Apparently, Murray witnessed it all and came home early from the expedition in shock. The girl is gonna work on Murray to get him to come in and give a statement."

The officers let out a small cheer.

"Don't get too excited, Murray isn't in yet."

"But what if Francis saw it too?"

"What if he didn't? I don't want to take any chances. Now, find out when the flight is landing and get in contact with the Football Intelligence boys to see when they are going to the airport. If they're going to pull in some of the faces ask if they'll pull in some of Jones's firm including Francis so that we can get his statement. But make sure they don't pull Jones. I want that pleasure."

"Yes, Guv."

Sharon put the coffees on a beside cabinet and switched on the bedside lamp.

Kevin woke up and stretched his tired body. "What time's it?"

"About seven."

"Seven o' clock!" Kevin was surprised he'd slept so long.

"Yep. Here's a coffee." She handed him a mug and sat next to him. "Do you want anything to eat?"

"Nah, not hungry. Had a great sleep though."

"Good." She kissed his bare shoulder.

Kevin caught her eye and they smiled. He put his coffee down and took the mug from Sharon and put it down too. He untied her dressing gown sash and pulled the gown off her shoulders, allowing her to pull her arms out.

Kevin then gently ran his hands down Sharon's breasts and stomach. He watched her nipples harden at his touch. He pulled the duvet from under her and she lay down. He bent over her and teased her nipples with his tongue and fingertips.

Sharon couldn't do anything. She was a slave to Kevin's desires. He was better than Lee at making love to her. Lee was selfish. As long as he got his way he was happy. The number of times he left her unfulfilled! Kevin was so loving and gentle. She could feel her skin tingle as he ran his hands over her naked body, exploring everywhere. She could feel her vagina tingle as his fingers and tongue explored her.

She gasped as Kevin entered her. She pulled his head down to hers and kissed him. Their tongues met and entwined. Kevin raised himself up on his hands and Sharon ran her fingers down his muscled arms and back.

The more he thrusted the more pleasure ran over Sharon's face. "Kevin! Kevin!"

Her nails scraped his buttocks and he couldn't hold off any longer. With one final thrust he came, and Sharon wriggled around beneath him, her nails sinking deeper into his flesh.

"I think I'm falling in love with you, Kevin!"

He looked down at her and kissed her.

Lee sat through the flight in virtual silence. He was worried about Kevin. Why did the coppers always pick on Kevin and not him? *Bastards! They always lifted the wrong person!*

The seatbelt sign above his head lit up, but it didn't bother him. He hadn't bothered to unfasten his seatbelt during the journey anyway. In fact, he had barely moved at all. He looked out the window and could see the lights of his great city, and he smiled.

"'Ere Lee, we goin' for a drink when we get back?" Terry asked, leaning over from the seats behind.

"Dunno."

"What's up, mate?"

"Do what ever you want, Terry," Lee said angrily, ignoring Terry's concern. "Now sit down and get your seatbelt on before those stroppy hostesses come back again."

Terry tutted and shook his head.

"Still worried about Kevin?" asked Joe who was sitting next to Lee.

"Yeah. Why are coppers such fuckin' bastards, eh Joe?"

"Dunno, but I'm sure he's awright where ever he is."

"Yeah, he'll be a tough nut for the coppers to crack."

"Yeah," Joe replied.

And then there was silence, broken only by the captain's announcement that they had arrived at Heathrow.

DS MacKenzie and DC Collins stood to one side of the Football Intelligence officers. They had already told their counterparts who they wanted lifted and were happy to leave that to the FIU boys. They could see the passengers start to appear in the arrival lounge, and immediately the uniformed officers moved in.

"Oh fuck, it's the Old Bill!" Mike groaned at the thought of the coppers treating them like dirt.

"'Ere, some of them have got clipboards! What do you think they're for?"

"Dunno, Terry."

"JOHN HOWDEN!"

John felt a hand on his shoulder

"Watch the Armani, copper!"

"MIKE HUNTER!"

"What the fuck do you want with me?"

A blue arm pulled him out of the firm and behind the police line.

"Fuck's sake! What is goin' on?" Lee hadn't expected any of this.

"God knows, Lee."

"JOE FRANCIS!"

"Me? Why me? See ya Lee!"

"Fuckin' hell!" Lee stood and watched three of his firm being led away. He couldn't believe it. "Fuckin' coppers!"

"Lee, what's goin' on?"

"Dunno, Terry, but it's fuckin' pissing me off!"

"C'mon lads, get a move on," said one of the uniformed bobbies. "Have you not got homes to go to?"

"Smart cunt!" sneered Lee. "C'mon, Tel, all these coppers are making me sick!" Lee stormed out of the arrival lounge with Terry and Ian in tow.

"There goes Jones," MacKenzie said as he watched the Chelsea boys leaving.

"Doesn't look too happy, Sarge."

"Nope! It won't make 'im any happier when the DI lifts him!"

The two of them laughed as an officer from the FIU approached them. "DS MacKenzie?"

"Yeah."

"Follow me and you can speak to Francis."

CHAPTER NINETEEN

MacKenzie and Collins introduced themselves to Joe and the three of them shook hands.

"How can I help you?" Joe asked.

"Lee Jones."

Francis laughed and shook his head. "What about him?"

"Our Guv'nor wants him bad."

"Not surprised, he's an evil piece of work," Joe said, pausing to suck on a cigarette. "What do you want to know?"

"The stabbing last night. Was it Jones?"

"Yep, sure was. I wasn't close enough to get a good look, but I soon got the drift of what was happening when I saw the knife and the Germans backing off. I presumed Jones started it all."

"What about Kevin Murray? Was he there?"

"Yeah, I was with him. He was nearer to Jones than I was so he probably got a better view."

"Dammit, I was hoping you wouldn't say that."

"How?"

"Murray came home this morning and turned up at Jones's girlfriend's place and poured his heart out. The only thing is, we don't know if he'll do the same down at the station."

"So that's what happened to Kevin!" Joe said, smiling. "Jones has been hunting high and low for him all day. He thought Kevin had been nicked! He'll be well annoyed when he finds out his best mate ran out on him!"

"'Ere, Sarge, the Guv will like that one!" Collins said. "It'll be one way to make sure Murray comes to the station."

"Yeah, go and phone him with the good news."

DC Collins left the room to make the call. He noticed that the rest of Jones's firm were being released so he popped his head back into the interview room. "Better watch out, the others have been let loose."

"Right then, better make a move," MacKenzie said, gesturing to Joe to get up and go.

Joe slipped on his new Stone Island jacket that he had bought courtesy of the Met. "See you later then. If you need any more info call me first thing tomorrow."

"Will do. And thanks."

Francis followed Collins out of the room, but they then went in different directions. Joe jogged to catch up with Mike and John and automatically joined in the conversation about what had happened in the interview rooms.

"Kevin?"

"Hmm."

Kevin and Sharon were lying in bed after an evening of having sex in several different positions and places.

"What are you gonna do about Lee?"

"God knows!"

"He can't get away with it, can he?"

"I hope not. I could handle the rucks an' that, but killing someone is well out of order."

"Who else was there?" she asked, her head still resting on his chest.

"Everyone really. We got into a fight at some pub after the match. Lee had loads of Gerrys around 'im so

124

I went to help out. Then I saw the blade. Shit!" He pulled away from Sharon's embrace and sat up and rubbed his face with his hands.

Sharon sat up too and tried to look into his face. "Did no one else see it?"

"I think that undercover copper, Joe, might've. I dunno."

Sharon didn't want to push Kevin too hard, but she wanted Lee put away now and didn't care if she never saw him again. "You could always ask 'im."

"What?!" Kevin glared at Sharon in amazement.

"Well, if he did see it then, y'know, Lee will get arrested."

"And if he didn't he damn well knows I saw it so he'll end up askin' me! A bit of a stupid suggestion, Sharon."

"Not really. Think about it Kevin. If Lee can kill and get away with it he'll do it again and again."

"Are you askin' me to grass on my best mate? The geezer I grew up with?"

Sharon pulled her knees up to her chest and looked away.

"Well, are you?" repeated Kevin.

"'S'pose I am."

"I don't believe it! You must be mad!" He threw the duvet off him and sat on the side of the bed and started to pick his clothes up off the floor.

"I'm not mad! Just being sensible and I think you should be too!" She slid across the bed so she was behind him, but Kevin stood up to slip on his shorts.

"Sensible? Christ Sharon! I hope you look good in black!"

"How?"

He was buttoning up his Yves Saint Laurent shirt but paused to answer Sharon. "Cos when Lee finds out, he'll kill me and then you probably!"

"But he doesn't need to find out."

"How do you work that out?"

Sharon started to get nervous. She didn't want to anger Kevin any more because she was scared in case she lost him. "Speak to that DI Welsh. He could fix it for you. And there's Joe. If Lee finds out he's a copper, then he will think it was Joe and not you that grassed!"

Kevin tucked his shirt into his Calvin Klein jeans. He didn't say anything, but he was thinking about what Sharon was saying. Grassing Lee to the Old Bill. With what he knew, Lee would go down for a long time, and by the time he got out he could be long gone.

"Kevin?"

He looked down to see Sharon half wrapped in the duvet and the bedside light shining across her shoulders. He sat down beside her. "What about you?"

"What about me?"

"Say I did grass Lee, what would you do?"

"Go with you."

"But you'll 'ave to face Lee."

"No I won't, if I go with you and you explain to this Welsh geezer. I'm sure he'll be able to do something."

"You want me to do it, don't you?"

"Yeah, I do. It gets Lee out of the way and it means we can be together properly."

Kevin smiled and put his arm around Sharon's bare shoulders. "I don't know if I could do it. It's against all my principles."

Sharon snuggled closer to Kevin. "Don't think about it, just do it." She nibbled his ear.

Kevin turned and kissed her, but pulled away quickly. "Don't take my mind off it. I've gotta think about it!" He stood up and headed for the door.

Sharon knelt on the bed and panicked. "Where are you goin'?" she called after him.

"Don't worry, I ain't goin' nowhere. Just gonna get a drink and think. You better get dressed in case we 'ave to go out."

"Okay."

Kevin disappeared through the doorway. Sharon clambered off the bed and rummaged through her wardrobe. She hoped Kevin would come to his senses. She dragged out her Armani Jeans, Chanel jersey and some underwear. She quickly tied her hair up and sorted her make-up. She didn't want Kevin thinking about it too much because she knew how much loyalty there was between him and Lee.

She grabbed her handbag and turned to see Kevin watching her with his bag at his feet. Sharon smiled sympathetically and went to him, holding him tightly.

CHAPTER TWENTY

Lee came out of the bathroom with a towel wrapped around his slim waist. He was still worried about Kevin and the fact that there was still no sign of him. Lee was sure that if the Old Bill had nicked him he would get deported, and if that was the case he would surely be home by now.

He picked up his cordless phone from the small hall table and selected Kevin's number from the memory. He let it ring for ages, but there was still no answer. "C'mon, Kev mate! Where the hell are ya?!"

He switched the phone off and slammed it back onto the table. His face screwed up in anger. He went into the bedroom and chose a new pair of Stone Island jeans and a Ralph Lauren hooded top. Dressed and with his hair gelled, he went into the living room, picking up the cordless phone again on the way. This time he selected Terry's number to find out what the police had wanted at the airport.

"Hello?"

"Yo Terry, it's Lee. What happened? What were the Ol' Bill wanting?"

"They were askin' questions about all the trouble in Germany and about the stabbin'." Terry knew it was Lee that did it. They all did and they were impressed.

"What did you say?"

"Nothin'. Told 'em I didn't see nothin' and that I wasn't involved in anythin'."

"Good stuff."

"Any news on Kev?"

"None. I've been trying to call 'im ever since we got back, but there's no answer."

"Kev can look after himself. He'll be okay where ever he is." The words of sympathy stuck in Terry's throat. He was beginning to think Kevin had been lifted because he could remember when he was deported from Holland a few years ago. It was a day or two before they let him home. *Damn it, Kev will be the man of the moment again!*

"Yeah, I just wanna know where 'e is!"

"Listen Lee, when I was deported it was a couple a days before the Ol' Bill let me home."

"A couple a days! You're kiddin'?"

"Nah, seriously."

"Fuck's sake!"

"Lee, calm down!" Terry said, realising that what he had said hadn't eased Lee's mind at all. "Do ya wanna go out for a drink tonight and we'll see if any of the other lads know what's happened to 'im?"

"Nah, gonna go over and see Shaz. Give 'er a present, y'know." He smiled at the thought of shagging the living daylights out her. Back to normal though. He'd take a dominating role again and she'd do what he told her to.

"Ah, right! Enjoy yourself. I'll call you tomorrow, yeah?"

"Yeah, see ya Tel."

He got the phone to dial Sharon's number. It rang and rang. *Where is she? She knew they were all coming home today! Bitch, she could've stayed in for him!* The anger rushed over him. *Damn it! Where is everyone?*

Lee went on to phone the rest of the firm, but still no one had seen or heard from Kevin. He tried his number again, but still no answer. *Stuff it!*

He picked up his house keys and went out to their local pub, knowing someone would be there. The rest of the firm would probably end up down there too. He tried Sharon's number one last time from the pub, but still no answer. *Fuck her!*

CHAPTER TWENTY ONE

The big grey brick building stood in front of them. Even at that time of night all of the lights were still on. A couple of beat coppers walked past them, laughing about some drunk they had dealt with earlier on.

"I dunno about this, Sharon," Kevin said, pausing on the steps.

"C'mon, Kevin. She linked her arm through his as he looked up and down the building. "Y'know it's for the best."

"I can't face speakin' to that DI Welsh. He's a cocky bastard."

"But you're gonna be helpin' 'im! He doesn't 'ave anythin' on Lee unless you tell 'im! So he's gonna 'ave to play it your way!"

"Maybe I should have called my brief, just in case like. Don't want to be stitched up or anythin'."

"I'm sure it'll be fine. If it does get a bit tough you can call 'im. Now, c'mon." She pulled him up the steps to the front office. She pushed the door open and pulled him through.

The duty sergeant looked up at the couple and tried to guess what they wanted.

Kevin paused.

"Kevin?"

"You ask for 'im cos I can't bring myself to do it."

She smiled and let go of his arm and then headed towards the sergeant.

"Yes, madam, how can I help?"

"DI Welsh, please."

Blimey! CID! These kids must be hot property. He had them down for their car being stolen. "And you are?"

"Sharon Gillespie and Kevin Murray."

The sergeant was sure the lad was a Chelsea hooligan, but couldn't be sure. He had seen and charged so many of them. "Just take a seat and I'll get him for you. Sam, look after the desk - I'm off up to CID."

A young WPC came through and sat at the desk and smiled at the couple. Sharon smiled back, but Kevin just glared at her. Just the thought of volunteering himself to the filth made him feel sick.

"Are you alright?" Sharon asked. "You look a bit strange."

"Just being here makes me sick."

She patted his thigh and smiled up at him, but he just stared ahead.

The sound of a door opening made them both look around. DI Welsh stood in the doorway. "Sharon, Kevin. If you follow me . . . "

Kevin didn't move.

"Kevin, please!" Sharon whispered and urged him to move.

Reluctantly he stood up and followed Sharon through the door.

The three of them were sat in one of the drab interview rooms when a PC brought in some coffees and put them on the table.

"Now, I'll have to speak to you separately and the interviews will have to be taped," Welsh said.

He knew he had to be polite to the yob, at least to his face. Without him there would be little chance of charging Jones and making it stick.

"What about protection against Lee?" Sharon asked.

"Well, this lot will take some time getting through so you'll be safe here."

"What about afterwards?"

"Have either of you got relatives or friends you could go to?"

Kevin didn't answer.

Sharon looked at him and held his hand under the table. "I've got a sister in Essex that might put us up, why?"

"Well you two can go there and we'll get you police protection if necessary. Now, your sister will have to be made aware of the situation and as long as she agrees, we'll be okay."

"I'm sure it'll be fine. She's never liked Lee."

"Kevin, is that all right with you?" Welsh asked.

Kevin just looked at him without replying.

"Kevin?" Sharon tightened her grip on his hand.

"Yeah, should be okay. What about my job? Can't jack that in."

"Could you take some holiday leave?"

"Dunno, maybe not straight away."

"You may have to phone in sick until we can sort something out," suggested Welsh.

"Can't do that! I'm up for a promotion and I ain't gonna blow it on nothin'!"

Welsh glanced at Kevin's file and noticed that he worked for a top marketing company. He couldn't understand how a football thug held down a high-powered job like that. Welsh couldn't care less

133

about Kevin's promotion chances anyway - all he wanted was to nail Jones. "Okay, I'll think on it. Once I've spoken to you both and decide what to do about Lee, I'll decide what to do about you, alright?"

"S'pose."

"If you don't mind, Sharon, I'll speak to Kevin first. I know how much he dislikes being here. Isn't that right, Kevin?"

"Don't push it, Welsh," Kevin said angrily. "I don't have to be here!"

"Kevin!"

"It's alright Sharon, I ain't going nowhere. I'll speak to 'im, just to get it over with."

The PC opened the door and Kevin noticed him eyeing Sharon up as she walked out. "Keep your eyes to yourself, copper!"

Sharon looked around and saw the PC's face go red as he looked to the ground.

"Now, now, Kevin, keep calm," Welsh said as the door closed. "This won't hurt, honest."

Kevin waited until Sharon was out of earshot and he leant forward, across the table. "Listen, don't get smart with me you bastard! Don't forget, I can leave at any time and there ain't nothin' you can do about it!"

"I haven't forgotten. But don't you forget, I've got enough on you to get you charged with assault, inciting a riot, drug dealing - and that's just for starters."

The two of them glared at each other, neither of them backing down.

DS MacKenzie entered the room and immediately felt the tense atmosphere. *This is going to be a long night!* he thought to himself.

* * *

Sharon was shown to another waiting room and a WPC popped her head in. "Would you like a coffee, love?"

"Yeah. You probably don't have anything stronger."

"'Fraid not," replied the WPC. "I'll be right back."

Sharon sat down and sighed. She thought about what would happen after all this was over. With Lee out of the way, she and Kevin could move away, get new jobs, get a house and possibly get married. She smiled at the thought of walking down the aisle with Kevin on her arm. She was imagining the dress she would have and the colour her bridesmaids would wear when her thoughts were interrupted by the return of the WPC.

"Here you go. Do you smoke?"

Sharon shook her head.

"I know why you're here. You're a brave girl."

"Yeah, if we get away with it."

"You should be all right. Welsh is a good copper. He'll look after you."

Sharon sipped the putrid vending machine coffee and the two of them sat in a silence broken only by the odd piece of small talk.

CHAPTER TWENTY TWO

Lee sat at the end of the bar while the rest of the firm laughed and joked about their exploits with England. It wasn't long before the pub was full of Chelsea lads, all talking about the same things.

"Hi Lee, doin' anythin' tonight?"

Lee looked up from his bottled beer and saw Tracy batting her eyelashes at him. "Dunno, I'll let y'know."

"Okay then, honey."

Slag, but a good ride, he thought to himself. *It's always good to keep a few on the go.* He went over to the payphone and tried Kevin's number and then Sharon's. But still no answer from either of them.

"Oi! Lee! Didn't think you were comin' down tonight!" Terry said when he spotted Lee over at the phone.

"Changed my mind. Thought I'd better keep the little lady waitin'. She'll be desperate by the time I get to her!"

Terry laughed. "Kevin?"

Lee shook his head. "Doesn't look like anyone else has seen 'im."

"As I said, Lee. He'll turn up in a couple of days when the coppers let 'im go."

"Why Kev, eh?"

"Must've got careless and got caught."

"Yeah, stupid bastard!"

"Yo Lee! How's it going?"

"Awright Joe, tried to call you earlier but you were engaged."

"Had to phone my Mum," he replied with a grin. "She worries about me!"

"Aw, ain't that sweet!"

The lads laughed and Joe joined in. *Yeah, laugh you mugs. Won't be long before you're behind bars.*

"How did you enjoy your first trip away?" Terry asked him.

"Excellent! Can't wait to do it again!"

"Yeah, it was a good trip this one, non-stop action. Mind you, not all foreign trips are that action packed, eh Lee?"

"Yeah, you were lucky this time, Joe. Landed yourself a good one."

"Still no sign of Kevin?" Joe asked.

"Nah, we reckon 'e's in the process of getting deported. So 'e'll probably turn up tomorrow."

Deportation? That's what you think! With any luck he's down the station telling all! "Deported, eh? Wicked!"

"Yeah, not bad. Mind you, it means he can't get into Germany again and it could be dodgy for 'im in some other European countries."

"It's just the thought of having DEPORTED stamped on your passport!"

The firm laughed again and Terry ordered up another round.

"Well, that seems to be everything. Thanks. Interview terminated at 23:28." Welsh switched off the tape recorder. "Thanks, Kevin, you've been a great help. I think you deserve a drink."

"Yeah, well I ain't gonna say what you deserve! Anyway, what happens now? Like when Lee finds out?"

"I don't think we'll need to tell him until it goes to court. What you've told us just fills in the gaps that Joe Francis and Ian Smith know. So with any luck Lee won't figure out you're involved."

"When do you think it'll go to court?" Kevin asked, wanting to get it out of the way as quickly as possible.

"Not too long I hope! Once we get a statement from Lee all the paper work will go to the CPS, and with the way public opinion is demanding tougher action against violent crime, it should go to court pretty fast. That's when Lee will find out. So be prepared!"

"Listen, I know Lee and I know what 'e's capable of, so I can look after meself!"

"And Sharon?"

"And Sharon!"

Kevin got up and headed for the door, but the PC just looked at him. "Look, copper, I ain't under arrest so I can come and go as I please! So move it!"

The PC looked at Welsh who just nodded his head to allow Kevin to leave the room.

Sharon lifted her gaze and her face lit up when she saw who was coming into the room. "Kevin!"

She went to him and hugged him, her head resting on his chest. "Oh Kevin, you've been ages! Are you alright? How did it go?"

"Alright, I suppose. Told him what he wanted to know. Hopefully I won't need to speak to the bastard again tonight - I'm sick of the sight of 'im!"

Sharon looked up at him. She was going to kiss him, but he pulled away when he heard Welsh's voice in the corridor. He turned and glared at the copper.

"Now Sharon, you'll be glad to hear that we won't need to speak to you tonight. Young Kevin here has told us everything. The only thing is, it's a bit late to take you down to Essex. Is there anywhere you can go tonight?"

Kevin shrugged his shoulders and looked down at Sharon.

"Kelly!" Sharon suggested.

"Who?"

"Y'know, Kelly. She's the one Lee tried to pull one night until he found out she was a friend of mine!"

"Oh her! Do you think she'll mind?"

"I'll have to call her," Sharon said, looking to Welsh.

"Well, if you follow me I'll show you a phone you can use."

"Thanks. Kevin, just wait here - I'll be back in a minute."

It wasn't much more than a minute before Sharon came back. "It's okay, she's making up the sofa bed for us."

"Great," Kevin said, picking up his holdall.

"DI Welsh has organised a car to take us there. "

"Not so great."

Sharon giggled and hugged Kevin again. Kevin smiled and backed Sharon out of the room and towards the front office.

"There they go, the two love birds!"

"Now, now, Sergeant," Welsh chided. "Those two have just solved all my problems. Now, let's get organised. We've got a thug to pick up!"

The pub was full of drunken Chelsea fans who were laughing, joking and singing.

A bell rang through the noise "Last orders! Last orders!"

A stream of orders were fired at the busy bar staff. Lee propped himself at the end of the bar again and leered at Tracy. He had tried again and again to call Sharon, but she wasn't there. *Well, that was her loss.* Tonight, he had his eye on a busty and randy barmaid.

Tracy looked at Lee and winked. She took a deep breath at the thought of rolling around with Lee again in the flat upstairs.

The bell rang again and the manager came out from behind the bar and started to clear the empties. "Come on lads, time to go home. We'll be open bright and early in the morning!"

Most of them left happily, but there was always the odd one who went out of his way to be difficult. The manager was used to that though, and expertly edged the problem cases outside.

"Lee, wait for me outside," Tracy said.

"Sure, babe." Lee pinched a fleshy backside and the owner flashed a cheeky grin before turning back to her work.

He staggered out the door and leant against an outside wall. His mind wandered over Tracy's body and what he was going to do to her. He couldn't wait to slip between her thighs. *Sharon's loss not his! Where was that supposed girlfriend of his? Must've got the hump about him going to Germany. But she knew he had to go. He was the leader of the best firm in England and he had to keep his reputation intact.*

Hope Kev gets back soon. Gotta find out what happened to him. Good ol' Kev, gettin' deported!

A hand wandering across his groin made him turn, and his eyes lit up when the flat keys flashed in front of him. He grinned and grabbed Tracy in a rough embrace, kissing her fiercely. His tongue penetrated her mouth as he started to grind his throbbing penis into her crotch.

"Lee! Slow down!"

"C'mon, Tracy. You wan' it as bad as I do!" He started to suck on her neck and his hands tried to open her jacket.

"But not 'ere!" She pulled away from him and headed for the stairs that led the empty pub flat.

Lee followed her closely up the stairs and he shoved his hand up her short skirt, grabbing at her bare pussy.

Tracy ran the rest of the way to the front door and fumbled with the locks. Lee stood behind her, rubbing his erect penis up against her buttocks.

They burst through the front door and Lee slammed it behind them. They greedily stripped each other's clothes off and Lee pushed Tracy against the cold hall wall.

Her fingernails tore into the wallpaper and her nipples went hard as she was pressed against the cool wall, Lee thrusting into her from behind. His hands grabbed the bouncing breasts and squeezed them.

Tracy started yelping with pleasure as she approached orgasm. All of a sudden Lee pulled away and Tracy twisted around. The look of desperation on her face made him smile. He reached out to her and pushed her to her knees. He then pushed her face to his manhood, her tongue working quickly as Lee climaxed.

She grabbed his buttocks and made Lee kneel in front of her and she pushed him over. Tracy crawled over him until her sodden vagina was over his face. She gasped as Lee's tongue teased her clitoris. She pulled away slightly and changed her position so they were licking each other to orgasm . . .

By the end of their rough love making they were both covered in carpet burns, but Lee didn't care. Tracy was a bit of a slag, but she was a good ride and did anything he wanted. And that's all he wanted from a bird.

CHAPTER TWENTY THREE

Sharon looked over at Kevin as the streetlights lit up his face. She tried to hold his hand, but he didn't respond. He just rested his head on the car window. She wondered if they had done the right thing. By the looks of Kevin, they hadn't.

She felt terrible - it was all her fault! She had split up two good friends. What was Kevin going to do without Lee? They were inseparable, and had been for many years. But Kevin had her now, and she would look after him. They would move away, she was sure Kevin would get another job easily enough, and so could she. Maybe they could go abroad, Spain or even the States. A voice disturbed her plans.

"Sharon? Sharon?" It was a WPC in the seat in front of her.

"Hmm, yeah?"

"Is this the place?"

"Yeah, yeah it is. Kevin we're here." She shook his arm and he looked at her blankly. She felt like crying.

As they clambered out of the car the WPC said, "A car will come and collect you tomorrow. But I think the DI will call you first."

"But he doesn't know the number," Sharon replied, reaching into her handbag for her address book.

The WPC smiled. "The DI knows everything!"

"Oh. Well, thanks."

"Don't thank them, Sharon!" Kevin glared at the two officers inside the panda car.

143

Sharon looked up at him and all she could see was hatred. She looked away and headed towards Kelly's flat. Kevin followed, his mind in turmoil.

"Sharon! Kevin! You awright?" Kelly smiled and let them in, but her smile faded when she was Kevin's face. "Just go through, you know where Sharon."

"Thanks, Kelly, we're not puttin' you out or anythin'?"

"No! Course not! Anything for a friend." She waited until Kevin had gone into the living room, and then grabbed Sharon's arm. "Psst, is Kevin awright?" she whispered.

"I dunno, I think so. I think he's a bit cut up about grassin' Lee to the police."

"Don't blame 'im. But 'e's done the right thing. Lee's turnin' into an animal. You'll be better off with Kevin."

Kelly was a loud Cockney girl, brought up in the East End and she knew how to look after herself. She always spoke her mind - and stuff everyone else. It was hard to believe she was a PA to one of the top advertising boffs in the city.

During the week she was dressed in Chanel suits and her hair was tied up, but at the weekend she let her hair down and she draped herself in Stone Island and Armani casual clothes. Saturday afternoons were always spent in Harvey Nicholls where she let her flexible friend do all the talking. And Saturday nights saw her heading for the trendiest of clubs.

She met Sharon years ago at an aerobics club they both went to. They had hit it off straight away and had remained friends ever since.

They joined Kevin in the living room and saw him sitting motionless, staring at the wall.

"D'you fancy a coffee?" Kelly asked. "Or maybe somethin' stronger?"

"Nothin' for me thanks. Kevin?"

Silence.

"I think we better get some sleep," Sharon said.

"Okay, I'll see you in the morning. Night!"

Sharon sat at Kevin's feet and looked up at him.

"Kevin? You awright?"

"Yeah. No. Fuck knows!"

"Wanna talk about it?"

"No, I don't really want to be reminded of that bastard Welsh!"

"I don't like seeing you like this."

"Like what? Fucked up?"

"Well, yeah."

"Neither do I. Never thought I'd do it. Voluntarily goin' into a police station to grass on Lee. Can't believe I did it!"

"It's for the best, really, it is," Sharon said, doing her best to comfort Kevin.

"Yeah, s'pose."

She rested her head on his knee.

"I thought we were gonna got some sleep?"

Sharon smiled and stood up. She went and turned off the main light, but left a small table light on in one corner. Then she started to undress.

"We haven't got anythin' to wear," Kevin said.

"Is that a problem? We're only going to bed."

Kevin smiled at Sharon and she grinned back, happy to see him smiling again. She neatly folded up her top and jeans, undid her bra and slipped off her panties.

145

Kevin sat in the armchair and watched her closely. She had a perfect figure. No cellulite on this babe!

Sharon noticed him watching her and took up a model pose. "You like what you see?"

"Yeah, I do as it happens!"

Sharon laughed and knelt on the sofa bed. "Are you not comin' to bed?"

"Yeah." He stood up slowly and started to undress, but he wasn't as careful as Sharon with his clothes. He just dumped them in a heap on the floor.

Sharon loved everything about Kevin. His well toned body, his dark hair and his eyes to match.

He slipped under the covers to join Sharon who immediately moved to be beside him. She was tired, but when she looked up at Kevin his eyes were wide open and staring at the ceiling. "You should try an' sleep," she said soothingly.

"Can't."

She slipped an arm around him and rubbed his shoulder.

"'Ave I done the right thing?" he asked, still staring blankly upwards.

"Yes! You have!" She propped herself up on her other arm and looked down into his face.

He looked up and tried to smile. "I bleedin' well hope so, cos life won't be worth livin' otherwise."

He wrapped his arms around her naked body and pulled her down onto him. Her long blonde hair felt soft against his skin and he ran his hand through it.

Sharon kissed his chest and ran her hand across it. "Once it's all over with, we can go away if you want."

"A well earned holiday, eh?"

"Well, I was more thinkin' about movin' away permanently."

"Eh? Where?"

"Anywhere! We'll just wait an' see, yeah?"

"Yeah."

He ran his hands down her body, and her back arched slightly and she sighed. Kevin kissed the top of her head. He was too tired and too mixed up to do anything else. Not that he didn't want to, he just couldn't.

Sharon's hand travelled further down his body, but travelled back up again when she heard a soft snore from Kevin. She smiled and settled down to sleep.

CHAPTER TWENTY FOUR

A loud crash and raised voices made Lee stir. He wasn't quite awake when two uniformed constables burst into his room, followed closely by a plain clothes officer.

"Lee Jones?"

"What the fuck do you want?" Lee replied, forcing his eyes open to see what was happening.

"Lee Jones, you're under arrest . . . "

"What the fuck are you on about?"

"You are under arrest. You do not have to say anything, but what you do say will be taken down and may be given in evidence against you in a court of law. Do you understand?"

"Who are you? And what do you want? Get your filthy hands outta my clothes!" He dived out of bed and grabbed a constable away, but immediately let go when he realised he was still naked.

The policemen tried to hide their sniggers as Lee hurriedly grabbed some clothes.

"For your information, I'm Detective Inspector Welsh, Fulham Police."

"You're the one who pulled up my mate Kev!"

"What of it?"

"You bastard!"

Further noises and voices from elsewhere in the flat made Lee more furious. "How many of you bastards are in here?" He barged past Welsh and into the hall just in time to see all of his scrapbooks, photo albums, diaries, and weapons disappear out of the front door.

"What are you doin'?"

"You're nicked, Jones, and you'll be going down for a long stretch for what I've got on you!"

Welsh was right behind Lee who spun around and tried to out-stare his enemy. "What are you on about?"

"You'll have to wait until I get you down the station."

"Guv!" The two of them looked into the kitchen and saw DS MacKenzie holding up a silver Stanley knife with CHELSEA engraved on it.

"What's this then, Lee?" Welsh grinned and examined the blade as it landed in a plastic bag.

"Looks like blood on the blade, Guv."

"Hmm, you could be right."

"Cut meself didn't I!" Lee offered unconvincingly.

"Did you now? We'll soon see. As long as your blood group matches the blood on here, you'll be okay. If not, you've had it!"

Welsh headed out of the kitchen and grabbed Lee on the way, and then dragged him out of the flat. When they got to the main door, bright flashes of the press cameras blinded them. Several microphones were shoved in front of them, hoping for a comment.

"Mr Jones! Mr Jones! Is it true you're the leader of the notorious Chelsea Casuals?"

"DI Welsh! What led you to Mr Jones?"

"Mr Jones! How did you become the leader of England hooligans in Germany?"

"Welsh! What are you looking for in the flat?"

"Mr Jones! Have you got any comments?"

"DI Welsh! Have you got any comments?"

Welsh pulled Lee through the pressmen and led him to the back of a waiting police van.

"How the fuck did they know what was goin' on?" Lee demanded.

"Your fifteen minutes of fame, Jones," Welsh said, looking at his watch. "You should make the breakfast TV news with any luck."

"Bastard!" Lee screamed as the van doors shut on him.

"Quick! Get the telly on!"

The bright light and Kelly's loud voice woke Sharon and Kevin. They rubbed their eyes as Kelly leapt across them towards the television and switched it on.

"What's goin' on?" a bleary eyed Sharon asked.

"Just watch, Shaz! Just 'eard it on the radio."

The screen came to life and the two breakfast TV presenters had solemn looks on their faces as one of them started to talk. "In a dawn raid this morning, a young man was arrested for alleged football hooliganism. Lee Jones of Streatham, South London, is a Chelsea follower and may have been involved in the violence that erupted in Germany last week. Marion Davies was there . . . "

The screen showed the outside of Lee's flat and pictures of Lee being dragged out to a police van.

Kevin's heart sank and Sharon's face was a picture of worry. "Oh my God!" she exclaimed.

"Couldn't believe it when I 'eard it!" Kelly said excitedly. "That's why I wanted to check the telly. Looks like they might try and make an example of 'im like they did the others a few years back."

"He better get locked up or else 'e'll kill me too!" Kevin said.

"Kevin, it won't come to that."

"Bleedin' well 'ope not!"

Sharon put a reassuring arm around him and rested her head on his shoulder.

"I better get goin'." Kelly stood up and left them.

Kevin lay back onto the bed and stared at the ceiling. Sharon looked down at him, she wished it was all over and they could get away somewhere now.

Kelly popped her head around the door. "Right, I'm off. Just let yourselves out whenever, okay?"

"Yeah, thanks Kelly."

"Help yourselves to breakfast and I've left towels out in the bathroom for you."

"Thanks again!"

"No problem! See ya!"

They heard the front door close behind Kelly, and Kevin pulled Sharon down to him and held her. Maybe Sharon was right. Maybe they should get away somewhere after this mess was cleared up. But it could be months yet. Between now and then it was gonna be a rough ride.

CHAPTER TWENTY FIVE

DI Welsh walked into the interview room and stood face to face with his enemy.

Lee glared at Welsh with a hatred that knew no bounds. He hated the police, always had done and always would do. He wasn't going to tell this copper anything.

Welsh on the other hand looked forward to informing Lee about what he had just been told by Kevin Murray, Joe Francis and Ian Smith. He knew everything there was to know about Lee, and he was going to make sure Lee would be sent down for a very long time. "Sit down, Jones. We've got a few things to talk about."

"Fuck off! I ain't got nothin' to talk to you about!"

Welsh sat down and lit a cigarette. "Suit yourself. I've got all day and I ain't planning on going anywhere. So sit down!"

"You aint got nothin' on me!"

"That's what you think. Now sit down!"

Welsh glared up at Lee as DS MacKenzie stood beside him and pushed him into his seat. Lee shrugged off the unwelcome hands and took a cigarette from the packet on the table. He looked around for a light, but couldn't find one.

Welsh held up his lighter. "Looking for this?"

Lee snatched the lighter from its owner.

"Now that you've settled in, let's get on with it." Welsh switched on the tape recorder and lent his elbows on the table.

Lee just stared at Welsh, determined that he had nothing on him. Welsh was just going through the motions like he did with Kev, and if Kev could handle it so could he!

Kevin and Sharon stood in Kelly's steamy bathroom. Sharon was slowly drying him off, secretly hoping he would make love to her.

Kevin took the towel from Sharon and wrapped it around his slim waist. He kissed her forehead, smiled at her and left the bathroom with the steam following him.

Sharon sighed, realising she was hoping for too much, and traipsed after him. When she got to the living room, Kevin was pulling on his jeans.

"Christ! Can't wait to get into some clean clothes!" he said.

"Yeah! And a good night's sleep."

"Company not good enough for you?"

"Oh Kevin, I didn't mean that! Just to get in a decent bed, that's all."

"That's okay then," he said.

They laughed and they continued dressing.

"Wonder what's happenin' at the police station?"

"Dunno Sharon, and I don't really care anymore!"

"He will get charged, won't 'e?"

"I dunno! Can we drop the subject please?"

Sharon looked over as he stood looking out the window. "I'm sorry."

"Looks like our lift is here. Are you ready?"

"Yeah, nearly. Just gonna leave a note for Kelly to say thanks."

"Good idea. You girls think of everything."

"Well, I'm not just a pretty face y'know."

"You're telling me!" He grabbed Sharon from behind and squeezed her breasts.

"Cheeky!" She finished the note and turned to face Kevin and they kissed.

A car horn interrupted them.

"Our lift?" she said.

"Yep, c'mon Sharon, let's go!"

Their journey took in their flats so that they could pick up some clothes for the days ahead. Kevin shoved his Yves Saint Laurent suits into a bag and cursed the way he had to treat them. He didn't care what that Welsh said, he was still going to work.

Sharon on the other hand decided to take some days off. Her boss was on holiday anyway and she never had much to do while he was away. Always ended up helping out one of the other secretaries.

The police car came to a halt outside a detached house in Essex.

"Bleedin' 'ell! Your sister lives 'ere?" Kevin was surprised by the size of the place.

"Yeah, smart innit?"

"Sure is! Her old man must earn a packet."

"Bank manager. Chrissie was able to give up work when she got pregnant."

"Not bad."

They climbed out of the car and watched it U-turn to make the journey back to London.

"Sharon! Sharon!"

Sharon spun around to see her sister half running down the garden path, and she smiled. "Awright, Chrissie?"

"Don't worry about me, what about you? What on Earth's been happening? Tell me everything and I mean everything!"

They laughed and gave each other a quick hug.

"And this must be Kevin?"

"Sorry, Chrissie. Kev meet my big sis, Christine. Christine meet my, er, new boyfriend, Kev."

Chrissie glanced at Sharon, but turned her attention to Kevin. "Kevin, just call me Chrissie."

"Thanks for putting us up at such short notice."

"No problem - anything for my wee sister! Now come inside and we'll get you settled in and then we'll get the kettle on and you two can tell me what's happened."

Sharon and Chrissie immediately slipped into general chattering and Kevin just followed after them with all the luggage. For what was supposed to be for a few days, Sharon seemed to have packed everything except the kitchen sink. *Why couldn't she have borrowed some of her sister's stuff?* Kevin thought to himself as he struggled with the cases. *Wasn't that the kinda thing sisters did?*

CHAPTER TWENTY SIX

"Sharon, are you ready? The taxi's 'ere!"

Kevin stood looking out of his living room window at the black cab below. He ran a finger around his shirt collar because it felt tight and uncomfortable. He looked around the room and he realised how much it had changed since Sharon had moved in with him. Everything was clean and tidy, and the furniture had been rearranged. He hadn't liked it when Sharon had first moved everything around - it was his place and his stuff - but after a while he had got used to it. And like she said, it did give them more space.

"Yeah, I'll be through in a minute!"

Sharon touched up her make-up and stood up. She looked herself up and down in the mirrored wardrobe. She had changed her outfit three times already and she still didn't think she looked right. It was too late now though. The taxi was here and Kevin would go mad if she asked it to wait.

She sighed and turned to straighten out the duvet. She smiled when she thought about when they had bought it and all of the rest of the stuff when she moved in. Sharon still didn't think Kevin had got over the shock of how much they had spent.

"Sharon?"

"Comin'!"

She picked up her handbag and headed for the living room, but Kevin was already in the hall waiting for her. She smiled at him and kissed him on the cheek. "Everythin' will be awright, you'll see."

"God, I 'ope so. Let's get going, better not be late."

The taxi journey was spent in silence. The driver had tried to make some conversation, but neither Kevin or Sharon encouraged him. They held hands and occasionally glanced at one another, but didn't say a word. They had said all that had needed to be said when they had stayed at Sharon's sister's place.

They had stayed there a few weeks when DI Welsh told them that he felt the situation had died down enough for them to get back to normal. Lee hadn't been granted bail because of the seriousness of the charges, and the German authorities were going through the motions of getting Lee extradited for the murder of the German youth.

The rest of the firm had been questioned too, and some of them had been charged with various things from mobbing and rioting to conspiracy to causing an affray. All of them, including Kevin, had been banned from Stamford Bridge for life. Not that it mattered as Kevin hadn't been back to the football since Lee had been arrested.

He did miss it - even the odd spur of the moment scuffles. Kevin always read the match reports in the Sunday 'papers though, so he still knew what was happening at the club he had supported all of his life.

When they decided that Sharon would move in with Kevin, their social circle changed. Sharon knew there would be gaps in Kevin's life where the football had been, so she talked him into joining a local leisure club. He wasn't keen at first, but then he discovered that when he was working out in the gym, he could vent some of his frustration that used to erupt at the football. They had also become members of a nightclub in Camden where they now went every weekend.

"'Ere we are, the Crown Court."

"Thanks, mate." Kevin got out the cab and held the door for Sharon. He handed over the fare and several pound coins. "Keep the change."

Kevin and Sharon looked up towards the imposing court building and looked at each other nervously. Kevin took Sharon's hand and led her up the steps to the main entrance.

"Ah, Mr Murray and Miss Gillespie! Glad you could make it!" DI Welsh was waiting for them at the top of the steps.

Kevin had got used to DI Welsh being around but he still didn't like him. "It better be worth it or else we've 'ad it."

"Cut and dried, just going through the formalities. Our friend will be going down for a very long time with a possible trip to Germany."

"He ain't no friend of mine," Kevin said.

"So how are you two getting on? Any sign of wedding bells?"

"Not that you'd get an invite. C'mon Sharon, I don't like to company we're keeping."

"See you inside!" Welsh called after them as they walked away from him.

"Bastard! I'd love to punch 'is fuckin' face in!"

"Kevin, calm down, please!"

He squeezed her hand and smiled down at her. "I can still dream!"

The courtroom was full, with most of the public gallery being filled with press people armed with drawing and writing pads.

Lee had glared at Kevin in the witness box, but Kevin had simply glared back, never once backing down. Now they were in the public gallery, all Kevin could see of Lee was the back of his head.

"All rise!"

The elderly judge made his way centre stage and sat down slowly. The rest of the courtroom took their seats again.

"Chairman of the jury, have you come to a decision?"

"Yes, we have your Honour."

"Chairman of the jury, do you find the defendant guilty or not guilty?"

Kevin and Sharon sat in a West End restaurant with a bottle of chilled champagne beside their table. The judge's voice echoed around their minds. "Lee Jones, I am sentencing you to ten years imprisonment. I am also authorising the German authorities to question you in connection with the murder of a German youth."

The press people had fought to get out of the courtroom, and as Lee was being led away he had glared up at Kevin. "When I get out, you better watch your back Murray!"

Kevin had remained silent and had directed Sharon towards the exit as the policemen pulled Lee out of the dock.

The waiter topped up their glasses

"A toast," Kevin said. "To the future. Our future!"

Also Available From S.T. Publishing

●**SATURDAY'S HEROES by Joe Mitchell**
128 pages with full colour cover.
Another debut novel, this time set in the world of football hooliganism.
Brilliant pulp literature in the tradition of Richard Allen.

●**THE COMPLETE RICHARD ALLEN VOLUMES ONE TO FIVE**
272-288 pages each with full colour cover.
Available again at long last, the classic Richard Allen novels that
charted the changing faces of British youth cults during the 1970s. In
Volume One, you'll find Skinhead, Suedehead and Skinhead Escapes.
In Volume Two, there's Skinhead Girls, Sorts and Knuckle Girls. And
in Volume Three there's Trouble For Skinhead, Skinhead Farewell and
Top-Gear Skin. Volume Four has Boot Boys, Smoothies and Terrace
Terrors. And Volume Five has Mod Rule, Punk Rock and Dragon
Skins.

●**ENGLAND BELONGS TO ME by Steve Goodman**
224 pages with full colour cover.
Superb debut novel set in the London punk world of 1977. The safety
pin might have been a fashion accessory, but the swastika was
something far more dangerous.

●**ONE FOR THE ROAD by Kid Stoker**
112 pages with full colour cover.
Debut novel by Kid Stoker of punk band, Red London. It tells the story
of punk band, The Outlaws, as they set out in a Ford Transit van to play
the pubs and clubs of Europe for one last time. *Crocodile Shoes*
meets *Auf Wiedersehn Pet*.

You can order any of the above books from wherever you
bought *Casual*. If you would like a free copy of our
illustrated mail order catalogue including latest releases as
well as the above titles, please write to the address below.
We send books all over the world.
S.T. Publishing
P.O. Box 12, Dunoon, Argyll. PA23 7BQ. Scotland.

As of September, 1996, we will be at a new address. If you want to contact us
before that date please write to the Dunoon address above.
After that date please contact us at
S.T. Publishing,
P.O. Box 12, Lockerbie, Dumfries. DG11 3BW. Scotland.